Lost in the Red Maze

Sameer Khan

VISHWAKARMA PUBLICATIONS VP

Lost in the Red Maze

First Edition - November 2016
© Author

ISBN - 978-93-85665-38-7

Disclaimer
This is a work of fiction, Names, characters, places and incidents are either the product of the author's imagination or are used fictitiously and any resemblance to any actual person, living or dead, events or locales in entirely coincidental.

Published by:
Vishwakarma Publications
283, Budhwar Peth, Near City Post, Pune- 411 002.
Phone No: (020) 20261157 / 24448989
Email: info@vpindia.co.in
Website: www.vpindia.co.in

Cover
Rosie Daswani and Pankaj Sapkal

Typeset and Layout
Chaitali Nachnekar - Vishwakarma Publications

Contents

1

6th of December 1992.

Asif met Sanju at Mahalaxmi Railway station. They walked towards Saath Rasta circle and entered the restaurant Ram Doodh Mandir. The restaurant was well known for its sweets and other Maharashtrian snacks. Asif looked at the wall clock that was placed above the manager's head. It was 4 p.m. Soon Asif ordered some *Misal*, and Sanju called for some *wada sambar*. It was a normal day but soon they felt ominous change in the air.

Some of the people in the restaurant began to talk in whispers with each other and started to leave. Asif and Sanju also left the hotel and moved towards Agripada, where Asif's uncle owned a shop. On their way they found that the number of vehicles on the road was diminishing and there were even lesser number of people on the streets.

They were meandering towards Agripada when things began to change drastically. They noticed that some police vans and jeeps were moving past them towards Madanpura. The moment they reached the center of Madanpura, they found that Asif's uncle's shop, along with most of the shops were already shut and the ones that were open were pulling their shutters down. Smoke was bellowing from a distance around Sagar hotel near Nagpada and many of the Bihari Muslim migrant squatters stood watching on the pavements outside their make shift slums with a terrified look on their faces.

Many young local Muslim boys stood on the street outside the shops in the center of the square and more began to converge. The crowd primarily consisted of young men and teenage boys. Asif and Sanju stood watching from the footpath. The boys in the mob were armed with stones and sticks and more people joined them. With every passing second tumultuous crowd began to swarm but nobody knew what was happening. An elderly Muslim old man tried to talk to the boys but was shooed away by them. It was total chaos and nobody was in charge of the growing mob. A cluster of jewelry shops on the street owned by Marwari Hindu businessmen had already shut down and just across the street were the Bombay Development Directorate or the BDD chawls, predominantly inhabited by the middle class Maharashtrian Hindus.

It was the day when a large group of right wing Hindus who had been agitating over the centuries old Babri Mosque had converged from all over India in city of Ayodhya, in the state of Uttar Pradesh. That day the mosque was demolished by the mob and as a fall out of the demolition, riots broke out between communities and Muslims and Hindus had clashed all over the country.

Some of the boys started throwing stones towards the BDD chawls and it was only a matter of time before few local police trucks arrived on the scene and along with them were the State Reserve Police Force. The boys began targeting the police vehicles and soon more police arrived on the scene. The presence of the police instantly resulted in the hostile elements among the mob getting further agitated. They began moving towards the police picket and started to throw stones at the policemen, as a result of which some policemen were hurt by flying missiles.

In the chaos, a short portly Muslim woman walked down from one of the chawls of Madanpura. She had rolled up her sleeves and wore a green dupatta around her head. The woman spoke loudly addressing the people that were watching from the top of their balconies, urging them to come down. The agitated woman thundered. "It is a matter of our honor." Not many people headed to her clarion call yet she continued urging them and screamed lividly, "Come down you cowards! They have broken our Babri mosque and you stand shamelessly like eunuchs. Don't you have any self-respect?"

The Muslim mob continued growing and there was absolute pandemonium, a few bearded elderly men now stood among the crowd but majority of them were young boys. The turbulent mob continued to swell in numbers and voices could be heard emerging out of the BDD chawls. There was a panic among its Hindu residents. Nobody from either side knew what was going to happen next.

The police sirens could be heard from a distance and soon police jeeps zoomed across the street from Agripada side towards Madanpura. The boys began to throw bricks and stones at the police jeeps, the stones hit the iron bars that shielded the glass windows of the jeeps. A few police trucks emerged from across the street towards BDD chawls and numerous policemen armed with double barrel rifles stepped out taking up positions by training their guns towards the mob. Before anyone could react the police opened fire without any warning. All hell broke loose and the mob ran helter-skelter as shots were fired from all directions. Asif and Sanju quickly ran and took refuge inside a shop that had its shutters half open. Sanju quickly pulled the shutters down and the fear stricken Bihari migrant worker inside the shop sat in one corner with his head between his legs.

Asif dragged a wooden stool and climbed on top of it. And from behind the iron grills, he began to peep outside.. There were a few boys lying on the streets, most of them were looking lifeless. One young boy who was shot in his back was still moving and groaning in pain. Shots were continuously being fired. Through the iron grill Asif watched bullets whiz all over the place. He looked up towards the tall building at the center of the square and was horrified at the sight. A boy aged around ten to twelve years was shot as he stood watching from his balcony on the third floor. His body just slumped to the ground.

Sanju was worried and he tried to prod Asif in an attempt to ask him to climb down. Asif jumped below the stool and sat on the floor, the Bihari migrant worker sat shivering in the corner in fright with his back to the wall behind the wooden partition. Thirty minutes had passed since the firing had commenced, yet they could still hear shots being fired. Asif looked towards Sanju and for the first time he could see fear in his eyes and his trembling hands. Sanju was a Hindu trapped in an overwhelming Muslim locality in the middle of a communal riot. Asif gently pressed his shoulders in a bid to assure him and a tearful Sanju buried his head on his shoulders and began to cry. They had inadvertently got ensnared into a precarious situation and their future looked uncertain. They were unsure if they would get out of this situation.

They sat motionless for a few minutes. The firing had died down with the exception of an occasional burst of gun fire similar to the crackers that are burst after some days following the end of Diwali festival. Suddenly there was an absolutely stunning silence for some time before suddenly the Azaan echoed from the local Mosque. Asif climbed the stool once again. The Azaan had an uncanny effect upon the policemen. They did not know what to expect after hearing the Azaan and in their morass began to withdraw.

Asif could hear sound of some trucks starting. The Azaan was still on while some policemen began climbing on back of the trucks and others started to move towards BDD chawls. By the time the Azaan was over there were hardly any policemen left on the scene. There was an eerie silence on the deserted street. Asif did not have too much time to think. Either they could wait for things to settle down, which was rather uncertain or they took a chance and escaped towards Saath Rasta. He peeped one more time outside the grill there was not a single soul on the streets. He peered down towards a stunned Sanju who sat absolutely frozen. Asif impetuously jumped down and pulled up the shutter with one hand and motioned Sanju to run with another. Sanju raised his head and was left completely bewildered. He had no choice but to run along with him.

They jumped out of the shop and started running towards Saath Rasta with full force and as they ran they witnessed what was left of the aftermath of the mayhem that had followed the protests. Bodies were strewn all over the roads but not everyone was dead, some injured were moving but there was no one to attend to their injuries. Asif ran faster and as a result Sanju was left behind and could not match strides with him. He slowed down a bit to allow Sanju to catch up but his slowing down caused an alarm amongst the migrant squatters living on the pavements. The migrant women panicked and began to scream. There were all sorts of voices emerging from the huts some called words like Police, poleese and other words that sounded like incomprehensible gibberish.

They continued running till they reached Saath Rasta circle. It was a neutral territory that divided Hindus from the

Muslim areas. Most of the shops in Saath Rasta were also shut by now; they reached near Behzaad restaurant and found out that there were absolutely no vehicles on the streets. Free India medical store and some other shops had their shutters half down. The news about firing in Madanpura had not yet reached there. Some people stood in the alleys near the market. They entered their neighborhood. Asif could see Ramya standing along with some of his cronies. It suddenly struck him that he was a Muslim in a predominantly Hindu area and his life could be in danger. He had stopped running but was still gasping for breath. He looked towards Sanju who was also out of breath yet there was a certain degree of ease on his face.

Asif felt a very palpable mistrust in the manner in which people saw each other. He could sense fear in the air and everyone looked towards the other with suspicion, or was it is his own paranoia? Most of the people in the locality were known to him and had grown up there but at that moment he went through a strange feeling. He felt as though everyone looked at him with mistrust. And it took a long time for wounds to heal and lives to go back to normal.

Growing Up

Asif belonged to one of the few Muslim families that lived in an overwhelming Maharashtrian locality. He had never felt any different from the others. As a child, he played cricket the whole day along with rest of the boys of his neighborhood. Rafiq was the only other Muslim boy in the locality and though they both were in the same cricket team yet he never got along with him.

Being the captain of the cricket team Asif would often arrange friendly matches with Prem Nagar, the neighboring locality. When they were in their early teenage years they started to play cricket matches for prize money. All the eleven players would contribute twenty-five paisa each, leading to the sum that would be two rupees and seventy-five paisa. Each time they would collect that amount before the match and whichever team won the match would win that amount. So it was like a double or nothing bet and this money was the ultimate grand prize.

There would be cricket matches on weekends between Asif's team and Prem Nagar cricket team. The captain of Prem Nagar was Tiwari who was a couple of years older to him and his best friend. Interestingly in spite of the rivalry with Prem Nagar whenever there was a match with any other team both the teams would unite as one. In case the match was fixed by Prem Nagar then the match would be captained by Tiwari and the team players chosen by him. Likewise, if the match was fixed by Asif's team he would be the captain and select the team players. Interestingly their own differences would be set aside when faced with any outside team.

Asif would celebrate all festivals with his friends. The Ganesh Chaturthi festival was celebrated with great fervor for an entire ten days. Ganesh idols would be placed in many homes and though it was primarily a Maharashtrian Festival yet even the non-Maharashtrian Hindus would also celebrate it. It never occurred to Asif that he was a Muslim or that the Ganesh Festival was a Hindu Festival. Every boy of his age would visit all the houses of neighborhood where Ganesh idols were placed. The poorer Hindus kept the idol for a couple of days while the affluent ones for entire ten days before immersing it into the sea. All the kids would go from house to house singing bhajans and prayers or the *"Aarti"* as it is known. The first house was that of BK Krishna, a Telugu speaking plumber who had a *Dhol* placed next the Ganesh idol that was a big attraction for Asif.

The Aarti would start as *'Jai dev, Jai dev Jai Mangal Moorty, Sri Mangal Moorty'*. Asif had learnt the entire Aarti just by attending various Aartis in every house in their neighborhood. Every home would serve different Prasad and libations. B.K Krishna often served a type of south Indian sweet as Prasad, some would serve Pedas and others would simply serve coconut pieces mixed with sugar or jaggery. It never occurred to him that he was any different from rest of the children of his neighborhood.

It was not just the Ganesh festival but his favorite festival was Gokulashtmi also known as Govinda. An earthen pot would be placed at a certain height tied by ropes from both sides to buildings and trees. Inside the pot there would be yogurt and coins, besides that, currency notes would also be placed around the pot as the grand prize. The boys would form human pyramids to break the pots, attempt multiple times, fall and rise again. The spectators standing around would throw balloons filled with water to make it difficult for the boys to break the pot. Asif and his young team would scamper on the ground for coins that would fall from the broken pot from the top.

Usually it would take three to four rings of people to reach the pot and the person who would reach the top would generally be a lightweight kid. Asif had once joined the pyramid and had been allowed an attempt to go on the top and break the pot. He did manage to break the pot but the pyramid had lost its balance and as a result of being on the top of the pyramid he had a nasty fall which resulted in a fractured hand. That was the abrupt ending of his short career as a Govinda pot breaker. Asif's parents never allowed him to join the pyramid again and he had to merely find solace in throwing water balloons like others.

The first time he ever felt the difference between him and the rest of the children was when he once got mocked by few bullies at school. It was a day when India had won a cricket match against Pakistan at Sharjah. Asif was celebrating with other children in the recess when he was accosted by some of the older boys. They had punched, kicked and jeered at him calling him a Pakistani. He did not understand the reason why he was subjected to such inhumane treatment. He had watched the match with his parents and had been praying and had even offered namaz when India had won the match. It took him some time to understand the reason he was singled out. That incident had left a huge impact on him and that was his moment of realization, something that never occurred to him before. He realized he was different.

Asif's grandparents had originated from Mangalore city in the state of Karnataka. Asif would visit them every summer vacation. His grandfather after spending most of his adult life in Bombay had retired to his roots and settled down in Mangalore. He built a huge house on his ancestral land and started Pineapple plantations on it. He also got three reluctant daughters married in Mangalore after raising them in Bombay.

Asif had many cousins but he remained his grandfather's favorite, doted upon and mollycoddled by him. His grandfather was very fond of Asif's playfulness and enjoyed listening to his Bombay accent. Asif would often play in pineapple farms the entire day and would follow his grandfather wherever he went. He was also loved by most of his relatives.

As a young boy he was in love with nature and would spend time running over the mud fences that separated the pineapple fields from the paddy fields. He was fascinated to watch his grandfather grow a number of fruits and vegetables in their farm that included Jack fruit, cashew nuts, coconut, sweet potatoes and a host of other fruits and vegetable. He loved spending time in Mangalore and would be completely crestfallen when his vacations would get over and it was time to return to attend the new academic year of school, which usually began in the month of June. As audacious as it may seem he would return to Bombay alone in trucks owned by any of his relatives.

His tryst with Mangalore suffered a huge jolt when suddenly one-day his grandfather suffered a cardiac attack. He was admitted to the Manipal hospital where he lived for a few days before death snatched him away. The death of grandfather effectively put an end to all of Asif's Mangalore sojourns. It was after a gap of five years, when he had appeared for his matriculation exams, that he went back to Mangalore, his native place. A lot had changed in those years that had passed. He was no longer a small kid but a sixteen years old teenager all set to go to college. The beautiful orchard and pineapple farms that his grandfather nurtured with so much devotion had withered into wilderness. The cow was no longer tethered in the cowshed. While a few remnants of old memories remained, most of the glory had faded. The well that once drew sweet water was no longer in use, its water contaminated and undrinkable. The coconut trees that his grandfather had planted stood withstanding the test of times like Pharaoh's pyramids. Asif turned gloomy seeing the condition of the farm. It was a pale shadow of the memories that he had stashed in his heart.

The ancestral home that his grandfather had built with such devotion and nurtured like a child till the time he was alive was now a complete mess. It was a ghost house; the walls had lost their paint and cobwebs ruled all over the roof. He went towards the bathroom and was glad to find that the "Maat" a huge cauldron made of copper that was used to warm water was still intact. Outside the bathroom lay a pair of wooden pair of slippers which belonged to his grandfather.

Before he returned back to Bombay, Asif decided to meet his cousins and visit their homes. The game of chess had become a rage among his cousins and all of them were hooked on to it. The chess fervor was not just confined to the young cousins but also extended to the older members of his family. Asif himself was a decent chess player but was an aggressive player and lacked the patience.

He was one week into his Mangalorean sojourn and decided to meet his youngest aunt and other cousins who lived in the nearby coastal town called Suratkal, which was an hour distance from his ancestral village. He left for Suratkal at noon and reached late afternoon. The cousins had just returned from school and were overjoyed to see him after years. In no time they brought out a chess board to impress him of their chess abilities. Asif was impressed with the chess skills the kids possessed. He got to know from them that their father and his uncle, a rather boisterous wise guy was one of the best chess players in the family.

Asif was eager to have a chess duel with his uncle and rather ingenuously expressed his desire to his aunt. Later in the evening his uncle returned from office and was speaking to his aunt in the kitchen. Asif happened to walk towards the kitchen to fetch some water and he overheard them speak

"Asif wants to play a game of chess with you," said aunt to uncle.

"You mean he came all the way to play chess with me?" retorted uncle, "Alright, let me teach the "Ghati" a few chess lessons" he chuckled.

Asif was shocked to hear those words. He could never imagine being addressed as a "Ghati" by his own people. He had often heard this term being used at times in a pejorative manner against the Marathi speaking neighbors in Mumbai by the non-Marathi speakers but he had never thought someone could address him a "Ghati." He was deeply hurt inside and was not able to reconcile to the fact that his own family would brand him as a "Ghati." He was from Maharashtra and spoke decent Marathi. Yet, neither did he consider Marathi as his mother tongue nor he did he ever identify himself as a Maharashtrian and now it dawned upon him that his own family labeled him a "Ghati."

Asif went through a huge transformation that day, on one hand some of the hooligans in school had taunted him as Pakistani for being a Muslim but ironically his own relatives called him a "Ghati," because of the fact that he was born in Maharashtra. It was a turning point in his life. It was more painful for him to be called a "Ghati" than a Pakistani because his own people thought he was different. He was completely shattered and left his aunt's home the same evening for his grandmother's home.

His myth and romance with Mangalore along with his innocent memories were all but over. He wanted to return to Bombay as soon as possible. He had never felt a stronger bond towards his state and the neighborhood that he grew up. And now he was reborn and considered himself a Proud "Ghati". He began to identify as "Ghati". Yes I am a "Ghati", he told himself.

He wished to return back immediately but since his original plan was to stay in Mangalore for three weeks and his tickets had already been booked so he could not do anything to hasten his return. But before he returned he wished to visit his grandfather's grave. When his grandfather was alive he would visit many of the Sufi shrines all over Mangalore along with him. His grandparents were descendants of the Turkish Sufis from city of Bijapur which today is a part of Karnataka state but once was a part of the erstwhile Adil Shah Kingdom. His Sufi ancestors from Bijapur who had settled down in Mangalore were known as Turks in the neighborhood. But now all he knew was that, he was not a "Turk" but a "Ghati."

He decided to visit his Grandfather's grave and slowly made his way towards the graveyard which was situated a couple of kilometers away from his home on the hill slopes. He started to walk towards the cemetery through the narrow alleys among the greenery and coconut trees. He loved the smell of red soil and enjoyed watching Jackfruits hanging tantalizingly on the low branches. He picked up some mangoes that had fallen off trees as a result of incessant rains of previous night. On the way he noticed most houses had tiled roofs except for a few newly constructed "Terrace houses" as they were known. Most newly constructed houses were owned by Christians and Muslims that had found new prosperity working in Middle East.

Asif continued walking towards the graveyard, the spot where Shamshu uncle once lived now stood a splendid new mosque. It had pristine bright stones with a high minaret. It was different and opulent from the other mosques. He was walking past the edifice when his cousin Asghar stepped out of the mosque compound. He was a distant cousin and had been working in Saudi Arabia for some years.

He looked at him and called. "Hey! Asif. Where are you going?"

"I am going to the graveyard." replied Asif.

Asghar laughed derisively "Graveyard? Why on earth the graveyard?"

He despised the caustic smug on Asghar's face and answered, "I am visiting my grandfather's grave". Asghar's countenance changed and he began to lecture him on how visiting graves was against Islam and that it was a heretic act and how one should desist from visiting graves and cemeteries.

Asif had never heard such words before and they were Greek to him. He hesitated for a moment and pondered if he was doing the right thing but then remembered his grandfather's affection towards him and wondered, why should anyone lecture him on visiting and paying homage to his own grandfather, who he loved so much?

2

Asif ignored Asghar's rants and proceeded to walk towards the graveyard that was still some distance away. He made his way through an alley that was predominantly a Christian locality. The houses had Christian names such as Lords Villa or Vaz Cottage and most of the houses were owned by Catholics which was evident by the display of holy crosses, statues of the Virgin Mary and small idols of Jesus Christ placed on the boundary walls.

He meandered along admiring the homes but was distracted when his eyes caught the glimpse of young girl falling from her bicycle at some distance. He could only see her back as she came down crashing on the ground with a loud noise. Asif rushed forward to help her as she lay wailing on the ground with the bicycle on top of her. He tried to help her to get on her feet but she continued to cry on top of her voice. On a closer look Asif noticed that the girl was around fourteen or fifteen years old. She was wearing a red frock which was in tatters and she had a deep laceration on her legs with blood oozing out of her wounds. He tried to help her on her feet but she couldn't move. He picked up her mangled bicycle and placed it aside. She remained indifferent to Asif who stood in front of her. He tried to talk to her in an attempt to pacify and distract her but she did not respond to his attempts and wailed persistently. He stood there waiting for her to calm down and after a while the girl stopped crying and looked towards him.

"Are you ok? Where do you live?" he asked her in Hindi.

She did not respond but instead stared blankly towards his face. He repeated the question, this time in English, "Are you ok?"

She answered in a cracked voice and in heavily accented Konkani Mangalorean English; "I stay there", pointing towards a tiled roof house at some distance. Asif smiled at her and was glad that she was responding to him. He asked her to stay where she was and rushed towards the house to get help. The moment he reached the gates of her house a barking brown mongrel came rushing out of the house and continued to bark inside the compound gates. He tried to look inside but there was no one in the compound so he called out loudly "Is anyone there?"

A few minutes a later man wearing a half sleeve white vest and blue stripped lungi emerged out of the house and looked at him in askance.

Asif spoke to him in English, "Uncle your daughter has had a fall from her bicycle and she is injured over there," The man was impressed with the fluent English spoken by the young boy but at the same time was vexed by news of his injured daughter. He rushed out of the compound to see the girl lying on the ground. Asif followed him. On seeing her father, the girl began to sob once again and both of them exchanged some words in Konkani. Asif could understand most of what was being said because Konkani was similar to Marathi, the language of his native state Maharashtra.

The man lifted the girl in his arms and carried her to his house. Asif picked up the mangled bicycle and dragged it following them. The man rushed straight into the house. Asif placed the bicycle in the compound and waited outside. He heard the man call him, "Hey boy come inside." The man also spoke in heavily accented Konkani English. He stepped inside a simple house that had a Mangalore tiled roof and red stone marble tiles on the floor. On the wall was a picture of Jesus Christ preaching to the multitudes. The pretty girl lay on the bed with her father applying Dettol on her bruises by her side. "Come, sit down boy," said the man. Asif sat down on a wooden stool. The man introduced himself, "My name is Mr. Rodriguez and this is my daughter Jenny. What is your name young man?"

"My name is *Asif*," he replied.

There was a subtle change in the man's countenance, his amiability suddenly disappeared but Jenny smiled at him. Mr. Rodriguez spoke after a pause, "Ok I will make some tea for you," so saying he went inside the kitchen and left Asif and Jenny alone together.

"So, Jenny do you go to school?' Asif asked with a smile on his face. The girl's eyes were still swollen because of her tears. He marveled at her lovely face and thought she was beautiful. She had light blue eyes which looked even prettier with them being puffed up.

"I study in standard nine. What about you?" She asked curiously.

"I just appeared for my board exams," he replied, and before he could ask any further questions Mr. Rodriguez returned with some tea and banana chips in a tray.

"So, where is your house? Where do you stay?" asked Mr. Rodriguez sipping tea,

"I am the grandson of Mr. Husain and I live in Bombay" answered Asif.

Mr. Rodriguez said with a smile. "Husain Turk. He was a good person". It was a small town so it was not surprising that almost everybody knew each other.

Asif finished his tea and Mr. Rodriguez rose up saying, "Ok young man, thank you for your help," so saying he escorted him to the door. Asif quietly made his way towards the door but secretly wished he could speak with Jenny a bit longer. Reluctantly, he stepped outside the compound and once again the dog started to bark.

He had forgotten the fact that he was actually on the way to his grandfather's grave and resumed walking towards the graveyard again. He reached the graveyard but found it difficult to locate the grave. It had been years since he had first visited the place and now thick foliage and shrubs that had grown over the years covered all over the place. The burial ground on a verdant hill was full of grass and shrubs. He could not find the actual unmarked grave so instead he started to pray in the direction he imagined the grave would have been. His mind went back to the moments he would spend time playing with his grandfather, the way he was pampered like a prince under the patronage of his grandpa but suddenly in the middle of his thoughts Jenny's face flashed in his mind. He shrugged his head and felt ashamed and guilty. He apologized to his grandfather and God for having allowed such thoughts to seep into his mind in the middle of prayers and continued his prayers.

On the way back home he walked past Jenny's home and kept looking for her. The door was closed and there was nobody in the compound. Asif kept turning and looking towards her house and hoping to catch a glimpse of Jenny again but without any success. He felt he was getting drawn towards her. He passed the spot where Jenny had a fall and noticed a silver cross on the ground. Apparently it had fallen of Jenny's neck. He picked up the crucifix and kept it in his trouser pockets.

That night he tried to sleep but his mind kept going back towards Jenny. He wrestled with his thoughts for a long time and tried to shoo them away but they would return to him like a ghost invading his mind. He tried to think of other things but Jenny would return to engulf his senses, overrunning his heart. He was a helpless prisoner of love and was madly in love with Jenny. He removed the silver crucifix numerous times and looked at it every time he thought of her.

Asif had earlier noticed children that studied in her school going to school early morning near his house. He got up very early in the morning as he knew Jenny would also go to school and the only way for her to the school was behind his house. In all his puerility he climbed the top of roof and sat on the sloping brown Mangalore tiles looking for Jenny and also watching the girls and boys walk to school. Some of the passing school girls giggled at him but the boys were not amused and looked at him with contempt and wondered if he was a city clown. He watched every student that passed towards the school but there was no sign of Jenny. He climbed on top of the roof each day hoping to catch a glimpse of Jenny but she remained elusive. The fact was she did not go to school and spent the next three days in convalescence but unaware he continued climbing and waiting for her on the roof every day.

On the fourth day he sat waiting on roof and by now all the passing school children stopped paying any attention towards him and went to school walking in a bovine manner. Asif remained glued to the narrow road that passed behind his house. He finally saw Jenny with bandaged legs trudging towards her school in her blue school uniform and a school bag on her back. He observed that she wore beautiful long hair. She kept pushing back her hair that dropped on her face. As she neared him and looked up towards him, she was amused to see Asif sitting on top of the roof like a monkey and burst into mirth. Asif felt embarrassed by her laughter and rather foolish for the fact that he was on top of the roof under sun. He looked down and smiled sheepishly. She smiled back and walked towards the school. Just a mere glimpse of her filled his heart with immense joy. For rest of the day he kept thinking of Jenny and her lovely face ruled over him. Her heavenly smile and blue eyes were an incantation and he couldn't wait for the next morning to have her glimpse again.

Next day Asif woke up early morning but he did not climb the roof, instead he waited outside his compound gate at the back of the house. After a regular stream of students had passed he noticed Jenny coming, she looked towards the roof looking for him and then proceeded to walk slowly looking at the ground, oblivious to him standing on the edge of the road.

He walked in front of her and greeted. "Hi Jenny!" She raised her gaze and cast her warm smile upon him sending waves of love cruising through his heart. He began to walk along with her.

"How are you now?" he smiled.

She smiled back and answered, "I am better."

"What were you doing on the top of the roof yesterday? Everyone thought it was so funny," she chuckled

Asif smiled sheepishly and replied, "I was waiting for you"

"Waiting for me?" She lowered her gaze and asked, "Why were you waiting for me?"

"I wanted to know if you were better and also wanted to see you"

A demure Jenny did not respond or look into his eyes but merely smiled and continued walking

"You live in Bombay, don't you?" asked Jenny

He answered "Yes. I live in Bombay but how do you know?" She smiled mischievously and said "Didn't you tell me the other day"

Asif smiled sheepishly. "Yes, I have been visiting Mangalore during my vacations." They went on to share their likes, dislikes. The conversation continued till the road forked and hit the main road. Asif's relatives lived around the corner and he could not risk them watching him with Jenny and thus had to turn back. Before that he asked her if he could meet her again. She didn't reply but instead smiled coyly and walked away towards her school.

Asif was over the moon. This was his first love and it was such a beautiful feeling. He did not know what love meant but it felt great. In all these years some of his friends had girlfriends but he didn't have any romantic inclination nor any feeling of love had ever germinated in his heart. He never shared that feeling towards any girl but now he was madly in love. The only name and face that ruled his heart and mind was Jenny.

He met Jenny again the next morning. His heart of full of love and it skip a beat every time her blue eyes met his. He wished he could hold her hand and speak to her till eternity but again they could only talk till the end of the road before he had to turn back, but those few minutes were the best moments of his life. He longed the entire day for spending those few minutes with Jenny. He would wake up early morning and wait for Jenny at the back gate. She always had a twinkle in her eyes when she saw him. They met for the next three days and those wonderful moments with Jenny were the best things that could have happened to him in all his life.

The next day Asif woke up early morning and plucked some fresh red roses from one of the last remaining rose plants in their garden, and presented them to Jenny who kept blushing as it was the first time ever anyone had gifted her flowers. Time froze as they looked into each other's eyes. They remained lost in each other but suddenly they were disturbed by a harsh voice in Konkani. Mr. Rodriguez stood next to them on a bicycle, "Jenny, what are you doing?"

She lowered her head and answered meekly, "I am going to school father."

Asif greeted Mr. Rodriguez, "Hello, uncle"

Mr. Rodriguez did not return his greetings and instead ignored him with contempt. He commanded Jenny to sit on the bicycle handle and quickly cycled away. Asif was embarrassed by the episode. He returned home and kept thinking of blue eyed Jenny. His young heart was full of love. He did not know what love was all about but his heart longed for Jenny all the time

The following morning, he waited for Jenny at the gate but she was nowhere to be seen. All the children walked towards school as usual. He anxiously waited for Jenny but watched in dismay as Mr. Rodriguez rode past him with disdain on his face and Jenny sitting on the front handle looking the other way. Asif kept looking at her as long as she remained in sight. It was a hard day for him. He was disappointed but continued thinking of her the whole day and wished Jenny had at least glanced towards him. The night was very long and he found it hard to sleep.

Next day, Asif kept waiting but again it was Mr. Rodriguez escorting Jenny to school. It dawned upon Asif that Mr. Rodriguez would no longer allow Jenny to go to school by herself. He watched them zoom past him. It was two days since he had spoken to her and it was getting very frustrating and painful for him to endure this trauma. His exam results were due and he had to return the next day. He just had one more day before he left and he wished that he could meet Jenny one last time before he returned to Bombay.

In the night there was a power failure and he lay on the bed in complete darkness. All kinds of noises were emerging from outside the house, sounds of nocturnal insects or an occasional cry of a peacock. It was the darkest night of his life. Every passing second was like a spear piercing through his heart. He got up from the bed and looked for some candles but could not find one. In the darkness he could see some glow worms through the window. Some had entered the house. He groped his way towards the door and was clueless about the time and guessed that it could be two or three in the morning. Asif got his hands on a match box near the door, opened the door and walked into the front yard, it was pitch dark outside. The moon was hiding behind the dark wispy clouds. The cool wind brought relief from the humidity. He walked towards the cowshed where there were many dry coconut branches, he pulled some of them and began to burn them.

The dry branches started to burn. As he lay on the ground he added some dry wood and dry grass to the bonfire, it stoked the fire. He enjoyed hearing the sound of dry burning grass which went kellick, kellick! The burning fire gave him warmth from the cold but his heart was burning with desire to meet Jenny one last time before he left for Bombay. It was his last morning there. He never realized when he had dozed off and was woken up early morning with the sound of Azaan from the nearby mosque. His clothes were a mess as he was draped in mud and morning dew. He quickly put some dry mud on the ashes of bonfire and went inside the house onto his bed.

He could no longer sleep. Grandmother came to call him for the morning prayers and seeing him on the bed went back to her room. He looked at the wall clock , an old antique clock that had a clay lion over the swaying pendulum. The lion had its mouth wide open as if mocking him. He remained awake and could sleep no more.

The sky was overcast and laden with rain. It was nine thirty in the morning, he could see children walk pass in school uniforms, some students carried umbrellas others wore raincoats and gumboots. It started to drizzle. Asif climbed on top of the house and sat on the sloppy tiles in the rains. He waited patiently, the rains continued to pour and he was completely drenched. The rain water rushed down from the tiles and he felt he would not be able to hold his balance. He climbed higher on the top and held on to the chimney for support. The rains got heavier, raindrops battered his head. He sat holding the chimney in rains while the students walked past him, some of them were bemused and others thought this boy from Bombay was crazy.

Asif did not bother about the funny or derisive reactions that he got from the students he just hoped that one of them would be Jenny. The rains pelted incessantly and there was no trace of Jenny. He kept praying that she would come alone and he could meet her and bid her good bye. The road stood deserted as most of the children had left and a dejected Asif remained glued to the muddy ground when he heard a bicycle go *tring, tring.* It was Mr. Rodriguez in his yellow windcheater racing his bicycle in the rains with Jenny sitting on the front handle wearing a pink raincoat. He held the bicycle handle with one hand and wiped the rain water from his face with the other. Jenny watched Asif sitting in rains and continued staring at him in spite of rains flushing in her eyes and remained glued to him till the point she could not see him anymore.

Asif stood on the roof and painfully witnessed Jenny disappear from sight. He was completely crestfallen. He had wished to meet her one last time but it was all over. In a few hours he would be in the bus returning to Bombay. He began to cry, his tears mixed with the rain drops. He could hear his grandmother call him and he slowly climbed down weeping. His grandmother stood near the cowshed looking at him and frowned "What on earth are you doing up there in rains?" Asif had no answer to her and his tears were indistinguishable from the rain water. She told him to dry himself and he quickly made his way inside without saying a word, knowing if he spoke his voice would crack or he would burst into tears.

He went and sat in 'korsi', which was the smallest room of the house, when he heard his grandmother call him for breakfast. He dried himself with a towel and looked at himself in the mirror. He could see his eyes were puffed because of tears and wondered if his grandmother would find out that he has been weeping. He quietly joined her on the dining table. She had prepared "chilla or Neer dosa" for breakfast with coconut chutney along with fish curry of previous night. He ate silently with his eyes lowered.

"What do you think you were doing on the roof in rains? No one does that. It's not funny." chided his grandmother. Asif remained muted and continued to eat with his head lowered. Grandmother pushed the steel glass filled with tea towards him and said, "After breakfast go to the bazaar and buy some cashew nuts and banana chips to take home with you."

When the rains had stopped Asif made his way towards the bazaar; some of the shopkeepers were his relatives, others acquaintances.. He walked inside one of the shops owned by one his relatives and bought some cashew nuts. They exchanged niceties and greetings and the shopkeeper asked him about the wellbeing of his family but Asif's mind was focused on Jenny.

Her school was not too far from the bazaar and he just had couple of hours before he returned to Bombay. Impulsively he started to walk towards Jenny's school, Holy Rosary Convent School. It was a mere ten-minute walk from the bazaar. Fortunately, when he reached the school compound there was no watchman or guard manning the gates. He sneaked inside and noticed that unlike his school in Bombay that had many floors this school was instead a cluster of tiled roof rooms on the ground. He could hear the chatter of students coming from the class rooms. Some children chanted in Kannada the local state language while the other voices were inaudible.

Asif waited under the mango tree inside the school compound. A peon walked towards a huge brass bell that hung on a tree and started to ring the bell that went tong, tong, tong, and tong. A huge roar of children followed and a swarm of students rushed out of the class rooms for the recess. He found himself in the sea of students wearing blue uniform. He stood among them completely incongruous like an alien, some of the children started to play around while others sat in circles and opened their Tiffin boxes. Every student had a different Tiffin box, all of different shapes and sizes. He looked around. There were mainly boys around him and some looked at him in a quizzical manner, others with inquisitiveness. Asif noticed most boys looked at him with suspicion and contempt probably aware that he was not a local but an outsider.

It was a small conservative town and though it was a co-ed school, mingling of boys and girls was not a common practice. There was a total segregation of boys and girls with boys sitting, eating or playing in one section of the ground while all the girls sat on the other side of the ground. Asif made his way towards the girl's section looking for Jenny. Most of the girls sitting in the ground found it very unusual and as a result some of the girls turned their faces way, others whispered into each other ears and giggled, there wasn't a single boy in the girl's section. Few girls with their squinted eyes accused him of blasphemy and their faces resonated imprecations. Asif stood highly embarrassed as a solitary boy without school uniform standing amidst a sea of girls, he felt like a complete pariah yet his love was driving him to search for Jenny. He kept looking for her among the hundreds of girls on the school ground.

Jenny was elusive; he looked towards the other side of the ground near the football field where some girls sat eating in circles. He walked towards the group but Jenny was not among them either. He was about to move to the other side when his eyes caught the blue eyes of Jenny who was sitting on the ground with two other girls near the goal post. She saw him and lowered her gaze. Asif dragged his feet towards her in spite of all his trepidations.

"Hello, Jenny. How are you?"

The two other girls sitting with her without saying a word abruptly got on their feet and just walked away leaving both of them alone. Asif stood in front of her while Jenny sat on the ground with her head down, both remained silent for a long time. He looked around and realized that they were under the spotlight from all sides. A large number of students looking at them from every direction, some gesticulated towards them and others merely laughed.

Finally, Jenny spoke. "Why are you here?"

"I…I came to see you Jenny!" he stammered.

"Please do not meet me again." responded Jenny rather curtly.

He stood there for moment looking at her and was speechless.

"Go away from here." she protested.

He was overwhelmed with emotions his voice cracked as he spoke "Jenny. I am returning to Bombay in one hour."

Jenny lifted her head briefly and looked towards a tearful Asif and slowly lowered her face again.

He spoke once again, "My results are due tomorrow. I shall come again next year. Will you meet me then?"

Jenny's eyes remained on the ground and she spoke brusquely.

I am never going to meet you again. My father hates you because he says you are a "Saracen".

"I am what?" he blurted.

"You are a Saracen," she repeated.

He had never ever heard that word before and asked her, "What does that mean?"

Jenny eyes remained glued to the ground as she spoke "I don't know but he told me you are a Muslim, a Saracen and I must not talk to you or else I will become a sinner."

Asif had no answers for such a statement and could not imagine how he should respond. He was at a complete loss of words and stood speechless for a while before he spoke, "Ok, Jenny. I am leaving. I just wished to say that, I love you." Asif looked at her with imploring eyes but Jenny did not respond or display any emotions and remained mum.

He had got her answer. He took a deep breath, exhaled and removed the silver crucifix from his wallet that he had been carrying with him all the while. He placed it in Jenny's hand, turned around and started to walk outside the school. He wiped his face with his sleeves. All the students in the school compound continued to stare at him, he kept turning back and hoping that Jenny would also look at him but she never did. As he walked out of the gates he heard cat calls and some school boys booing him. He did not cry but he was angry, very angry with Mr. Rodriguez for treating him in such a disparaging manner. What pained and broke his heart was Jenny's reaction. She had also spurned his feelings. He was sad when he was called a Pakistani, hurt when addressed as Ghati and now the girl he loved seared his heart by labeling him as Saracen. He left for Bombay and decided he would never return to Mangalore again.

3

It was late night when Asif and Tiwari returned home after a drinking session. A bedraggled Bablu stood at some distance outside Asif's house reeking of alcohol. Bablu was a sot yet a very likeable guy when he was not under the influence of alcohol but everyone knew that he also could be the most irritating person on earth when he was in a drunken state. He would often indulge in frequent brawls that ended up in fights but he had never misbehaved with Asif, not even when he was in his worst alcoholic mode. Asif nevertheless avoided him.

Bablu was of medium height, fair complexion and wore spectacles which he kept removing and wiping off his shirt regularly almost as if he was suffering from an obsessive compulsive disorder. A horrible alcoholic, the type of guy who would drink any type of liquor depending on how much money he had in his pocket, sometimes whiskey, beer and other times he would even drink country liquor. In situations when he was completely devoid of money he would often pester Asif for money by concocting some story or the other or find other ways and means of ingratiation to ask for money for liquor. Asif knew it was all a pack of lies and just means to waggle him of some money yet he would turn a blind eye to his antics and at times would willingly get fleeced by his fake stories and embellishments.

Asif stopped his bike outside the house. Tiwari noticed Bablu staggering towards their direction and walked away. Both belonged to the same caste and their families were from the same village in state of Uttar Pradesh but they always had issues with each other.

"I want to talk to you," stuttered Bablu.

"Yeah, tell me," answered a disinterested Asif

Bablu was known for exaggerating things and throwing in blandishments and he was fully aware of his antics, ignored him.

Bablu spoke again, "Asif, it's important."

Asif remained unimpressed and answered in a cursory manner.

"Ok, I am listening."

"Today an old man was asking questions about you." Asif was intrigued hearing about it and inquired, "An old man asked about me? Who was he and why was he asking questions?"

Bablu spoke again, "I don't know. I have never seen this man before, but he looks like *Anna* (South Indian man). He kept asking questions about you at the *naka* (street corner) this evening."

"What did he want?" asked a visibly perturbed Asif.

"I don't know, but it seems he has some important work with you," said Bablu trying to balance himself.

Asif wondered what the old man would have to do with him.

"What did you tell him?"

"I just told him that you are not around and you will return late, so he left"

"Did he say anything else?" quizzed Asif.

"No, he did not say anything but just said that he would return tomorrow," saying Bablu staggered his way home. Meanwhile Tiwari returned and asked in a rather condescending manner, "What was the "*bevda*" (alcoholic) saying?" It was amusing to note that he called Bablu a "*bevda*" when he himself was totally drunk. Asif chose not respond to him and bid him goodnight.

The following afternoon Asif stood outside Babu Bhai's restaurant. Babu Bhai was a Malayalee owner of the restaurant. This was a regular meeting place for Asif and his friends. It was an unusually noisy day, cars kept honking and he could also hear a loud speaker play loud music at a wedding at some distance. Tiwari was busy buying *mawa* from the paan stall outside the restaurant. He would often bully the paan vendor for fun and indulge in pranks like snatching a packet of *gutka* or eating a pan without paying for it. The paanwala who was a migrant would comply meekly without much of protest because he knew Tiwari did it for fun, not any malice.

While Tiwari was busy bullying the paanwala, Asif's attention was drawn towards a bespectacled quaint old man staring at him from the footpath across the road. He found it very unusual and was uncomfortable. The man's face looked familiar and he wondered if he had ever met that man before but could not recollect it. He ignored him and looked the other way but soon realized that the man was persistent and kept staring at him. It was highly annoying and something that made him very uncomfortable. He was increasingly peeved at the man's behavior yet preferred to ignore him.

In the meantime, Tiwari walked towards him. Asif suggested that they leave and proceeded to walk towards the bridge. No sooner had they walked a few paces that he heard a man call him in south Indian accent, "Aaseef!" He turned around to find the same quaint old man who had been staring at him. Tiwari looked at Asif with questioning eye raising his eye brows. Asif nodded his head in negative.

"Aaseef, I want to talk to you," said the man hesitatingly.

"Yes, tell me," answered Asif.

The man looked towards Tiwari and said, "Aaseef, I want to speak to you alone"

Asif gestured Tiwari, who went back to the paanwala.

The old man began to speak, "Aaseef, do you remember me?" Asif had no clue about the man and shook his head in negative.

The man's eyes moistened and he spoke with a cracked voice, "I am Mr. Rodriguez from Mangalore."

A tumultuous wave of emotions swept Asif's heart. It was almost six years and he had never returned to Mangalore since his painfully agonizing departure. He stood numb and was at loss of words and could not imagine that he was facing Mr. Rodriguez an imperious man who detested him so much. He had forgotten the man's face but now his memory was afresh. He realized Mr. Rodriguez looked much older than he actually was and his face had turned darker with many more freckles and wrinkles on it. Asif saw his blue eyes and remembered Jenny. She had inherited his deep blue eyes.

Asif gathered his composure and said, "Hello uncle! How are you?" A doleful Mr. Rodriguez dropped his shoulders and started to weep. Asif was dumbstruck and did not know how to react to the situation. People walking nearby watched them with curiosity. He instinctively said "Uncle, let's sit in the restaurant and drink some tea." He ushered him to walk towards the nearby restaurant. Mr. Rodriguez followed him to the restaurant like a Zombie.

There were a few people inside the restaurant and Asif chose to sit in the furthest corner as there were no customers sitting around that table. The manager of the restaurant Abdul looked at him, nodded and signaled the waiters to switch on the fan. The waiter reached for the switch and glanced at them with intrigue. The cacophony of waiters ordering food inside the kitchen and Abdul ringing the bell to ask for the amount for bill remained unchanged.

Tears kept flowing from Mr. Rodriguez's eyes and he continuously wiped them with his handkerchief. Asif discerned that the insular person that he once remembered him as had been replaced by a broken man sitting across, facing him. It was an unbelievable transformation of a man in six years. It appeared as if he had aged two decades in those years.

Asif was perplexed at his behavior and could not understand the change. He let him settle down for a while and offered him some water and spoke, "Tell me uncle, what's the matter?" Mr. Rodriguez drank some water gathered his composure and spoke, "Aaseef, it's about Jenny."

Asif felt a painful pinch in his heart when he heard Jenny's name, his throat ran dry. As he reached for the glass of water, he asked, "What about Jenny?"

Mr. Rodriguez looked into his eyes and his voice cracked as he spoke, "Jenny is lost." and once again burst into tears.

A wave of emotions crashed through Asif. He waited for Mr. Rodriguez to pause before he asked "Jenny is lost? Lost where?"

Mr. Rodriguez lowered his gaze and spoke in choking voice, "Jenny was never the same after the day you left. She would remain aloof for hours. She had changed a lot." Asif interrupted "But uncle, it was so many years ago…."

Mr. Rodriguez didn't pause and continued speaking, "She barely spoke to me for all these years. Some months ago she just disappeared, I kept looking for her, I even lodged a police complaint but there was no trace of her and last week I got a call from her. She was in great fear and said that she had left the house to find you but someone had trapped her and tricked her and now she is in a brothel in Bombay in a place called Grant Road."

Asif felt his head was spinning and the walls were going to crash on him. Mr. Rodriguez began to sob loudly. "My child who had never left the confines of our village is now in a brothel in this city" Asif was shell shocked and completely befuddled but he gathered his composure and spoke,

"Did Jenny tell you where she was in Grant Road?"

"No, she was about to speak more but her phone got disconnected. I don't know where or in what condition she's now." Saying this, he broke into sobs once again. Asif asked him, "Did you inform the Police?"

"No. I cannot tell the police. I cannot let the world know my daughter is in a brothel or that she is a prostitute." responded teary eyed Mr. Rodriguez.

Asif could not believe what he was hearing. He was in immense pain and the pain got aggravated listening to the foolish values of Mr. Rodriguez and his vacuous fears about aspersions that would be cast upon his daughter's character, he wanted to argue with him but thought otherwise seeing incessant tears flowing from Mr. Rodriguez's eyes.

Asif was in such a state of trauma that he wanted to scream, bang his head on the walls yet he maintained his composure, Mr. Rodriguez had come with hope and he could not show weakness to a distressed father.

The pain in his chest was getting unbearable, he was in a state of stupefaction, hotel manager Abdul watched Mr. Rodriguez weep and wondered what the matter would be and so did the rest of the restaurant waiters who looked with intrigue towards them.

After a while they walked out of the restaurant and stood silently outside the restaurant for a long time before Mr. Rodriguez spoke "Aaseef, I am leaving for Mangalore today."

Asif could not believe his ears, it was clear that Mr. Rodriguez had abandoned Jenny and had no intentions to pursue or search for her nor did he ask Asif to do so. He was simply escaping from the situation and was more concerned about the ignominy faced by his family. For him his community and the shame of his daughter being found in a brothel after escaping was more of concern regardless of the fact that the guileless girl, his own daughter had been deceived into it.

Mr. Rodriguez looked into Asif's eyes for a second before turning his face away. He pressed Asif's right shoulder with his left hand before walking away. Asif stood there watching Mr. Rodriguez walk towards the Mahalaxmi Railway station and disappear among the sea of commuters. He stood staring in his direction for a long time and wondered whether Mr. Rodriguez's inequity of asking Jenny to spurn his love was brutal or the fact that he was walking out of the situation was worse. He also lamented and was ashamed of the fact that he had obstinately been blaming Jenny for spurning his love and held a grudge against her but on the contrary she had loved him all those years and had now taken the audacious step because she loved him.

He was resuscitated from the traumatic thoughts when he heard Tiwari call his name across the road. He crossed the road and joined him on the other side

"Who was the old man?" inquired Tiwari. Asif remained mute.

Tiwari could sense that Asif was disturbed after meeting the old man and asked again.

"Who was the man?"

"An old acquaintance." he replied.

4

Finding Jenny was never going to be an easy task. Grant Road was a huge area and consisted of hundreds of brothels, some were well known but there were others that were lesser known and rather inaccessible.

Asif had grown up in an atmosphere that was filled with a panorama of all kinds of people and he was acquainted with some of the people that frequented the brothels. He had never visited any brothel, though he would often hear some acquaintances boast about their escapades and sexual prowess in the brothels. He would hear some of the boys speak of their discomfort and aversion to using a condom or the cap as it was known in the street lingo. Asif never had the inclination or the desire to visit any of the brothels. He went to a decent convent school and was well aware of the pervading new dangerous disease called AIDS that spread due to wanton sexual dalliance. It had never occurred to him and he never imagined that he would ever step inside a brothel but fate had written a different script for him. He had noticed an occasional prostitute standing on the road in Kamathipura or markets near Grant Road where they would come to shop however he had never interacted with any prostitute.

He could not think of anything other than Jenny ever since he had met Mr. Rodriguez. Asif remained lost in his thoughts and wondered how he would locate Jenny in such a populous place and maze like Grant Road but his best bet was no other than his dear friend Tiwari who had been visiting brothels since an early age. He had invited Asif to join him to a brothel some years ago but after being politely refused had never pushed him for it.

He met Tiwari in the evening at usual. It was a Monday and Tiwari being a devotee of Lord Shiva would visit the Shiva temple every Monday evening and avoided alcohol owing to his weekly fast devoted to his favorite god on that day.

Asif accompanied him to the Temple and stood out as Tiwari entered the temple after reverently ringing the bell that was placed at the entrance. He returned after a few minutes with libations smeared on corners of his mouth. They entered the nearby *Matka* (Local illegal betting) betting center situated in the alley across the temple.

The *wada pav* seller who sat on his makeshift stool shared a smile with them. They walked inside and reached the end of the cul-de-sac. A huge black board hung on the wall with *Matka* results inscribed on it in white chalk. Next to the blackboard was a glass frame of goddess Laxmi, the goddess of wealth with a withered garland of marigold flowers around it.

Two men sat on a long wooden bench accepting bets with a confirmation slip on a colorful piece of paper. A bald man sat on a metal chair with an iron cash box accepting and paying money for bets placed and paying dividends for previously won bets. Tiwari placed a bet on number one and three for open and close for Kalyan Franchise of *Matka* betting and after collecting the betting slips walked out across to Moon Light restaurant owned by a man from Gujarati Chilia Muslim community. Tiwari signaled waiter to bring tea who in response screamed at the kitchen in his hoarse voice. Within minutes' tea arrived and Tiwari began to slurp tea in the noisiest fashion. The moment he poured the tea from cup into the saucer the second time Asif spoke,

"I wish to visit the *Adda* (Brothel)."

Tiwari who had lowered his face with his eyes focused on the saucer raised his head and narrowed his eyes.

"You want to visit the *Adda*?"

Asif nodded his head in affirmative.

Tiwari smiled and went on to finish the tea he had poured in the saucer.

"Mahatmaji, you wish to visit the *Adda*, Really? Wow!"

Asif went to outpour his painful love story, about Mr. Rodriguez's visit and the reason he wished to visit the brothels.

Tiwari heard him intently and his countenance changed, he drank some water from glass wiped his mouth with his right hand and spoke,

"Grant road is a huge place; it's got numerous *Addas* and thousands of prostitutes that live in the most hostile conditions. It will not be easy to find her."

"I am aware of it; just tell me will you help me?" asked Asif

Tiwari knocked the wooden table with his knuckles and said, "Alright, today evening I will take you there."

Both met that evening and took a taxi for Falkland Road. They alighted from the cab outside the Delhi Durbar restaurant situated near Peela house. Peela house, a word that was a hybridization of word play house which was founded during the British rule and was once upon a time host to many cinema halls and theatres. Tiwari led the way towards Shuklaji Street, an old section of Mumbai red light section. The street across was bustling with people. A number of cinema theatres were situated in a close proximity on the same lane. The movie halls built in gothic architecture had imperial names like New Roshan, Alfred, Edward, Royal, a legacy and remnant of British rule. The movies playing in the cinema were old and some as old as 1970s. Alfred cinema had a huge poster of the old Amitabh Bachchan movie Deewar. A movie, that was a classic but at least a couple of generations old, other cinema halls had raunchy eastern European movies. A large number of prostitutes were standing outside the cinema halls waiting for potential clients.

Asif dragged his gaze away from the raunchy women and followed Tiwari, towards the Shuklaji Street, Kamathipura. It was called Kamathipura because it was home to a large number of Telugu speaking prostitutes and workers from the Telangana and Andhra Pradesh region. Numerous prostitutes dressed in Sarees and blouses exposing their midriff and others wearing nightgowns and ostensible make up, stood outside the brothels and sidewalks facing the main road, making lewd gestures and verbally inviting prospective customers, sometimes using words seductively like, "*Chalta Kya?*" and when the man would pass by ignoring them, would throw profanities at them like, "*Saala Kam ka nahi hai, Uthta nai kya re?*" (Useless fellow, do you have a problem in getting an erection?)

They walked brushing their shoulders against other men on the busy but squalid street when Tiwari suddenly and slowly turned his face towards Asif, winked and said. "You see this road?" It's called *Safed Gully* (White lane) During the British days it was the home to white prostitutes, *Gori Chamdi*, white skin not all this desi stuff.

Asif had never been to that part of the Mumbai city and had been blindly following Tiwari like a blinkered horse, ignoring the noises and lurid spectacle around.

Tiwari entered one of the lanes towards the brothels of Shuklajee Street. Some of the buildings were colonial structures with names like G-9 and No 25. Tiwari slowed down and whispered into Asif's ears, "We are entering a brothel called 007."

A large number of prostitutes stood at the doorway and inside 007. None of the girls appeared attractive. Tiwari held an increasingly tremulous Asif's hands and ushered him inside the brothel. A nervous Asif followed him hesitantly, once inside the brothel a young pimp of their own age, who was a rather good looking boy, came forward and walked towards them and said in hushed tone, "I will get you a real tight one, not here but in the Villa nearby." Asif pretended not to have heard and ignoring him continued to follow Tiwari inside the brothel.

The young pesky pimp persisted with his pestering and this time spoke a bit louder. "I will take you to the Villa. It is much better than this rotten place. No good flesh here, come with me." Asif continued to ignore him but Tiwari overheard the pimp's voice and turned around to glare at him. The young pimp promptly took few steps backwards and made his way outside the brothel vanishing from their eyes.

Asif was perspiring heavily due to humidity and consternations of being inside a strange brothel in red light area. Tiwari turned towards him and said, "You just stay here, right in this corner. I am going inside to meet Maharaja; he's an old pimp and will surely be of help." Tiwari did not wait for Asif's assent and quickly disappeared into a dimly lit room that had its door ajar.

Asif stood on the passage inside the 007 brothel biting his nails and wiping the emerging beads of sweat on his forehead with the back of his palm. Girls walked past him, in and out of the brothel, most of the girls glanced at him and tried to draw his attention. A few of them deliberately brushed against him as they walked past him but he avoided looking into their eyes or allowing them to get his attention. The moment he would look at any of the prostitutes they would start gesticulating or moving their eyebrows to allure him towards them. Almost all of the women had garish makeup on their faces and not many of them were attractive and at times it was difficult for him to distinguish between a woman and a eunuch, as apparently a large number of eunuchs dressed slovenly as women were also part of the flesh trade.

Among the few presentable girls were the young petite Nepali prostitutes that had their presence in significant numbers all over Shuklajee Street. Unlike the local Indian prostitutes that often got aggressive and went out of the way to draw the customer's attention, the Nepali girls kept to themselves and instead politely waited for customers to approach them.

All kinds of characters continued to enter and exit the 007 brothel and many of them were apparently drunk. Most men were alone but there was also a group of ostensibly drunk men that entered the brothel and created ruckus. The clamorous group of men stood teasing the eunuchs who walked away abusing them. The women stayed away from them maintaining a distance and did not abuse or interact with them. After a while the noisy men entered various rooms to have sex, leaving Asif the lone male standing in the passage.

Asif did not wear a watch and had no idea how long Tiwari had been absent. He was about to lose patience when he noticed Tiwari emerge from the dimly lit room and motioning him to walk out of the 007 brothel. Asif quickly followed the suit but had no clue what Tiwari had discovered inside the brothel. He was impatient but remained silent and waited till they reached main road.

They walked towards Peela House amidst the cacophony of noises of prostitutes, taxi horns and the annoying pimps that tried to gain their attention. Asif quickly asked Tiwari if he had got any information from Maharaja. Tiwari spat the tobacco from his mouth on the road and said, "Maharaja said we should try Kennedy Bridge brothel. There is no Mangalorean girl in Shuklajee Street according to him."

"Are you sure?" asked Asif

"Well we have to take his word. I believe the man. There is one pimp I am acquainted with at Kennedy Bridge brothel. We will have to try him. Maharaja feels he should be the right person to help us. I actually dislike the creep but we have to take chance upon Maharaja's input."

Tiwari paused to put tobacco in his mouth and continued "I know one pimp called Ravi *Dadhi* at Kennedy Bridge. The man earned the sobriquet *Dadhi* because of his beard. He is a real denigrate but well connected with all the brothels, pimps of Grant Road and beyond. I am sure if Maharaja believes it then he would surely be able to help us some way." Asif felt hopeful listening to Tiwari's words as the day ended.

5

They met once again the next evening and took a taxi to proceed towards Kennedy Bridge. After alighting they walked briskly to reach the end of the bridge and took a right turn towards an old building. Asif was alarmed to find a policeman in uniform talking to a cigarette vendor but the policeman was no mood to perform duty and was in fact drunk. Tiwari started to walk faster, the street was dimly lit with a cluster of buildings. Tiwari led the way quickly and entered one of the buildings. It was one of the old rundown buildings, the staircase made up of wood with some of the stairs missing due to which they had to occasionally hop while climbing.

There were hardly any lights on the staircase, as they began climbing the steps a strange noisome smell hit them. The stench got Asif to the point of vomiting but he maintained his composure and wondered what the origin of such putrid odor would be. They reached the second floor, it was a squalid place. Some women standing in the passage with heavy make-up instantly began importunately smiling and gesturing in their direction. Tiwari signaled him to wait outside and entered one of the rooms. Few girls on the balcony stood glancing at Asif but soon realized he wasn't interested in them and went on looking for other potential customers. Two other prostitutes standing close by also discerned that Asif was not interested in them and continued to babble with each other. A strong scent of Ponds talcum powder along with the fragrance of Jasmine flower garlands used by the girls on their hair hit his nostrils. It was a bizarre combination of Ponds talcum powder, Jasmine flowers and the brothel stench. After some minutes Tiwari emerged out of the room with a lean whitish man with stubble on his face wearing a yellow check shirt and black baggy trouser. Some of his shirt buttons were unbuttoned and he continued buttoning his shirts as he walked out of the room. The man was certainly not in very good mood at being awakened by Tiwari from his sleep.

Asif stood facing the man, the girls nearby continued speaking obstreperously in Telugu, the stubble man screamed at them, "*Idhar se jao, bhenchod,*" the girls left without a whimper of protest. The loutish man looked at Asif directly but spoke to Tiwari,

"*Aye, Bhaiya, yeh kon hai?* (Who's this man?")

Tiwari looked at him directly and answered ingratiatingly, "Ravi, he's a friend and he needs some stuff."

"Did you get money?" demanded the bearded man peering at Asif in an insolent manner.

Asif nodded his head in the affirmative.

"Ok, go down, I will return in a while." saying the man dashed inside one of the rooms.

They began to climb down stairs. Asif looked towards Tiwari in a quizzical manner and had not understood what was going on.

"I told him you want to buy some crystal meth, let him come down and we will deal," answered Tiwari in a hushed tone

They stood under the darker section of the Kennedy Bridge for Ravi Dadhi to arrive. After waiting for few minutes they could see Ravi Dadhi walk towards them. Asif walked further under the bridge where it was complete darkness. An impatient Ravi Dadhi pulled out from his pocket a small plastic pouch and handed it to Asif and in a very querulous manner demanded, "C'mon, now give the money."

Tiwari intervened facetiously, "Oh! Of course Ravi you will get your money but before that we need a small favor. Is there are girl named 'Jenny' in Kennedy Bridge or Grant Road?"

Ravi Dadhi got fractious and said, "What the hell is all this? Just give me my money and get lost you creeps."

Tiwari in a bid to mollify him said, "Yaar Ravi, we have a problem, kindly help us find this girl!"

Ravi Dadhi got flabbergasted and held Asif by his shirt, "Bastard, I want my money."

He held Asif by scruff of his collar. A pugnacious Tiwari intervened, "Ravi let him go."

Ravi Dadhi got furious and hissed menacingly, "Bhaiya, just give my money or both of you will pay for it dearly."

Asif meanwhile was able to get out of his hold and managed to push Ravi Dadhi who lost his balance and stumbled falling backwards. He tried to gather himself and lunged forward but Asif landed a forceful punch on Ravi Dadhi's nose. He was not a very strong man and with the hard impact of the punch was sent rolling on the dusty ground.

Ravi Dadhi realized that he stood no chance against two men and tried to escape but Asif caught him by his neck and pulled him to the ground choking his neck with his arms.

Tiwari came charging forward pummeled his face a few times and said, "*Bhadwa*, just tell us about Jenny or we else put your penis in your anus." Ravi Dadhi froze as he realized he was not a match to both of them and he could be badly hurt if tried to indulge in a physical dual.

It was time for Asif to take charge, "Sister Fucker pimp, tell us if you know anything about Jenny?"

The man was petrified and pleaded, "I don't know anything about any girl?"

Asif choked him harder making it harder for his to breath, and asked, "Bastard tell us about the girl from Mangalore."

Ravi Dadhi gasped for breath and replied, "Wait, wait! Please don't beat me. There was a girl in Grant Road from Mangalore but now she has been moved to Colaba at Salim Bhai's Adda."

Asif continued to hold him in tight grip and asked again, "Where is Salim Adda in Colaba?"

"It's at Gulf Hotel building, Colaba," gasped Ravi Dadhi.

Asif maintained his grip on Ravi Dadhi's neck and said, "Bastard if you are lying, I will kill you."

"No boss, I am not lying," he pleaded.

Asif loosened his grip a bit and that allowed Ravi Dadhi to scramble out of his clutches and he ran back towards the brothel without turning back.

Tiwari caught Asif's hand and began running in the opposite direction, Tiwari panted, "Asif let's get out of here before the pimp returns with his cronies," Asif was slow to react. Tiwari hollered "It's dangerous, let's get out of here."

They began running with full strength and continued running till they were out of breath and reached the main road. They looked back and found no apparent threat. There was nothing apart from some cars on the street. A taxi stood on the road with taxi driver sleeping with his legs dangling out of the back seat window. Tiwari caught his breath and got inside the front door and sat next to the driver's seat prodding him, waking him up from his sleep and asking him to drive. The animated driver who was half asleep got out of the back seat of the taxi and got into an argument with him meanwhile Asif opened the door and got in the back seat.

The taxi driver panicked and refused to drive. Tiwari slapped him hard across the face and said, "*Bhenchod,* do you know who's sitting behind?"

The driver was scared out of his wits and had no courage to ask any further questions and reluctantly started the taxi and began driving without asking any further questions or the destination. Tiwari's bluff had worked. They were soon driving towards Bhatia hospital and out of danger. Throughout the way the taxi driver kept repeating "Sir, I am a poor family man, please keep me out of it." Meanwhile they had reached Saath Rasta. They asked the taxi driver to stop and got out of the cab. Asif reached for his wallet to pay the taxi driver but the driver simply started the taxi and drove away.

6

Asif got out after the one-day cricket match got over. Tiwari was already waiting for him. Asif started the bike and they made their way towards Worli. Their first stop was Poonam Bar near Worli naka, after drinking a few pegs they stepped outside the bar with Tiwari pushing the watchmen away who tried to waggle for some tip.

They made their way towards the Worli Sea face, on the way they stopped at Himalaya Heights building and bought a bottle of whiskey from a wine shop. Soon they reached Worli Sea face, a number of people walked on the promenade, a few local residents were jogging along the sea side and a number of hawkers stood selling bhel puri, peanuts, coconuts and other eatables.

It was low tide hence many people sat on the rocks that were well inside the sea and others sat on the boundary wall. Tiwari had forgotten to get a water bottle or a cold drink to mix with whisky hence they bought two coconuts from a vendor and after drinking some water added whiskey inside the coconut. They slowly traipsed their way towards the rocks deep inside near the waves. It was a full moon night and the sound of waves made the night surreal, they made their way deeper in the beach, empty liquor bottles, used condoms littered the shore.

He felt seawater with his hands and having finished the whiskey threw the empty coconuts shells in the sea. Asif looked towards his watch and decided to leave. They reached the main road and saw a police van drive and stop near the beach. Some policemen stumbled out of the van. Most hawkers were migrant workers and started to walk away seeing the cops. Some policemen stayed inside the van while others sat on the boundary ogling at the women walking on the street.

Asif suggested to Tiwari that they should leave the place. He started his Yamaha RX 100 and raced towards Haji Ali. When they reached National Sports Club they could see the magnificent Haji Ali *Dargah* on the right. They got down the bike and sat on the sea wall marveling at the magnificent Mausoleum. It looked serene and beautiful on the full moon night. Tiwari started to recite some poetry in praise of Haji Ali *Dargah* and was arrantly immersed in his devotion towards *Dargah*.

Asif saw a car stop some distance away from the bus stop on the other side of the road, a woman in white salwar kameez stood on the bus stop.. The man driving the car stepped out and started to smoke a cigarette, placing one hand on the sea boundary wall. The woman moved like a gazelle towards the man. They had a brief conversation and the man drove away. The woman returned to where she had been standing. Her body language had changed, her shoulders were down and there was no trace of the gazelle walk.

They continued driving towards Colaba crossing Peddar road, Kemps corner towards Teen Batti. Tiwari tapped Asif on his back, "You know Jaggu Dada? Apna Jacky Shroff was a *Shana* (don) of Teen Batty." Asif snickered "*Saala he was a don of a posh area*," and they both burst into laughter. They reached Queen's Necklace, street lights were bright and there were many cars zooming on the streets, in a few minutes they reached Regal Cinema Colaba and made their way towards Gateway of India.

It was around eleven forty-five pm there were some hawkers on the pavements. Asif parked his bike on the footpath and sat on the Gateway of India sea boundary. An old Arab man dressed in traditional Arab garb walked past him, he was followed by a couple of Uttar Pradesh migrant hawkers conversing with him in broken Arabic, he exchanged a few words but did not buy any stuff from them, the hawkers returned grumbling in Bhojpuri dialect.

A peanut vendor walked towards them and Asif bought some peanuts from him. They ate peanuts and looked up towards the splendid Taj Mahal Hotel facing the sea front. They could see some *firang* (Caucasian) tourists standing and watching the waves from the sea facing suites that had their lights on but most of the other lights were switched off.

Some young apparently gay boys in their teens and early twenties sat on marble chairs near them. Asif glanced towards them but the boys were too busy to notice them. Asif decided to walk away and sit at some distance. A taxi drove past the gay boys, a portly Arab with curly hair sat on the back seat of the taxi. A couple of the gay boy walked up to the taxi and after exchanging some words, one boy sat in the front seat of the car next to the driver while another sat at the back. The moment the taxi moved forward, the boy sitting next to the driver winked at them as the car drove away.

They got up and continued walking towards the end of the road taking a right turn to enter the lane leading towards Arabian restaurant. The restaurant had already half shutters down, some people sat eating food inside. The half shutters meant customers were no more allowed in. A few drunkards stood eating at a *Pav bhaji* cart nearby.

Asif looked at the watch, it was half past midnight. A mobile *Pav bhaji* stall stood under the yellow street lights at some distance on the footpath. There wasn't much movement of vehicles on the streets. The nearby Hoodoos pub which was a famous gay joint was still open. Three young men who were not more than Asif's age stood outside the pub door.

The food stall vendor was busy serving *Pav bhaji* to other prostitutes who stood waiting. Three other men also stood eating *Pav bhaji* were least interested in the women. Another prostitute who stood at some distance stood singing an old Rajesh Khanna and Asha Parekh song, 'Tere Karan, mere Saajan'.

It was a completely new territory for Tiwari. He had never been to this part of the city. He had been a regular patron to the cheaper and older brothers of Central Bombay and red light places like Kamathipura, Kennedy Bridge, Peela house etc. but Colaba was different. It was a much more up-market place and beyond his domain. People of Colaba were much better dressed and often spoke English and likewise the prostitutes of Colaba were also better and expensive than their Grant Road counterparts.

Ravi Dadhi had mentioned Gulf Hotel building but it was not an easy task to locate the actual brothel. There were numerous flats in the building and not all were involved in flesh trade and any wrong move could get them into trouble.

They stood waiting next to the mobile Pav Bhaji cart. The three women after eating Pav bhaji and failing to find any customers disappeared in the adjoining dark alley. The perfume showroom was still open and so was Ideal restaurant. They walked across Gulf Hotel and noticed some men sat eating food. A couple of Arab men emerged out of the building and stepped inside the restaurant, one of them was tall with stubble on his face and wore a long flowing Arabic robe, the other was a clean shaven man wearing jeans. Asif got a hunch that they had probably emerged from the brothel yet it was a difficult task to locate the exact flat where the brothel was located.

Asif was glued to the building when his attention was drawn towards two young gay boys making funny gestures and attempting hard to catch their attention. One of them wore a tight green T-shirt while the other had a blue check shirt. Asif ignored them and tried to focus towards the building. It wasn't the boys' fault, they were in their own territory. Hoodoos was a well-known gay joint and the boys were merely trying to ascertain if Asif and Tiwari belonged to their own tribe. Asif ignored the gay boys and kept his attention on the entrance of the building but Tiwari got increasing peeved with their antics as they were inching closer by the minute.

"How long are we going to wait here?" snapped a distraught Tiwari.

The two gay boys were joined by couple of other boys who were slightly older and that diverted their attention giving some relief to Tiwari. It was two a.m. and there was just one solitary customer at Pav bhaji cart. The imbroglio continued for few more minutes, the two older gay boys left and the younger boys got back to do what they were doing earlier, trying to gain attention.

The restaurant was empty of customers, the shutter was pulled half down and only the waiters and other staff sat eating their meal. Some Arabs and Indians kept entering and exiting the building at regular intervals. Asif wasn't sure if it was the right moment to enter the building. The two gay boys meanwhile were inching towards them by the minute. Tiwari anxiously kept looking at his watch and waited for Asif to make his next move. One of the gay boys who wore a green T-shirt walked up to them and asked for the time.

Asif insouciantly looked at his watch and replied Fifteen minutes past two. The green T-shirt boy smiled and went back to his partner who wore a wrist watch in his hands. Tiwari got increasingly restless by the green T-shirt boys move.

"Let's get out of here, before everyone on the street starts believing we are gays," protested Tiwari nervously.

Asif realized the situation was getting a bit precarious as the gay boys were growing bolder by the moment. To get out of the situation he decided to walk towards the Pasta lane away from the Hoodoos club much to the relief of Tiwari. They walked past shops that had names like Benhur and reached the petrol pump. The wine shop owned by the Parsi gentleman was surprisingly still open.

A tall beefy, rather intimidating African man with massive biceps who could easily be perceived as a drug peddler stood wearing khaki cargo pants and white T shirt outside the wine shop. He glanced at them and soon realized they were not business. He appeared to be waiting for someone and detested their presence yet he wasn't rude and spoke to Asif,

"You need some stuff?"

Asif shook his head in negative.

"What are you here for? Are you looking for a fuck?"

A nervous Tiwari did not understand the conversation and being immensely intimidated by the African man quietly stepped back.

The African spoke again, "You looking for a fuck? Tell me boy."

Asif smiled back and fearlessly assented, "Yes, I am looking for a fuck and I wish to go to the Gulf building."

The African liked his straight forward answer and took Asif's statement veritably. He pointed towards a gangly old man standing under the streetlamp across the road with two other apparent drug addicts and said,

"You see that man? Just meet him and he will take you to Arab building for a nice fuck."

Asif thanked him and dashed towards the grizzled old man. Tiwari had not understood much of the conversation but he was quick to walk away from the African.

The gauntly old man was pallid with deep clavicles and slanting eyes.

Asif did not utter a word but the old man had noticed him speak to the African, he merely raised his head and without wasting time Asif replied, "Gulf building."

The old man stuttered blithely, "Five hundred rupees, short time". The moment he spoke those words it became clear that he was not a drug addict but an alcoholic.

Asif pulled a ten rupee note from his pocket and placed in the old man's hands. That instantly got his attention and the old man started walking towards the Gulf building followed by Asif and Tiwari. They once again walked past Hoodoos. The gay boys were no longer present. The old man teetered into the stygian building that had massive wooden steps and even though they tried hard to walk tiptoe and stifle the noise, every time they stepped on the steps it resulted in a loud cracking noise.

They reached the second floor and stood facing a massive wooden door. The old man waited for them to settle down before ringing the bell. He pressed the bell but there was no response, he waited for some time before prodding the button once again. Someone peeped in the keyhole from the other side of the door. The old man stepped forward in front of the key hole to give a better view to the person watching from inside.

The door opened and a man who was around forty years of age, medium height stood facing them, the old pimp greeted him "*Salaam*, Salim Bhai," a man with a dense moustache attuned by merely nodding his head. The thick moustache man whom the old man addressed as Salim Bhai led the way inside the flat towards the drawing room. There were at least four massive rooms with a large king-size bed in each room and the doors were decorated with colorful curtains.

Salim Bhai led them towards the last room. He merely shook his head signaling them to move towards the sofa and make themselves comfortable before leaving the room. Asif reached for his wallet, checked for money and realized that he had only four hundred rupees with him. It was an expensive brothel and the old pimp had already quoted five hundred rupees for short time. Raising his head, he peered at Tiwari and asked, "How much money do you have?"

Tiwari lifted his eyebrows, pushed his hand into his trouser pocket and retrieved some currency notes of hundred, fifty, twenty and ten rupees' denominations.

Asif asked in hushed tone, "How much?"

"I need to count," fumbled Tiwari.

Asif whispered in snappy manner, "Please Tiwari, hurry up; we shouldn't appear as impecunious rag pickers."

He counted the money which was three hundred and seventy rupees.

That meant only one of them could go for a short time. Without uttering a word Tiwari shoved the currencies of various denominations in Asif's shirt's front pocket.

Salim Bhai entered the room; he was followed by a string of women of all ages and sizes, older women wore saris and younger girls wore T-shirts and skirts and some of them wore night gowns.

There were at least ten women in the room. He took one glance and realized Jenny wasn't among them and wondered if there are other girls in the brothel. He cleared his throat and asked.

"Are there more girls?"

Salim Bhai raised his eyebrows and signaled someone who wasn't visible to them but stood outside the room. Within minutes six more women entered the room, some older women, three in their twenties and one teenaged cadaverous girl with swarthy complexion. Jenny wasn't among them too. He wondered if there would be more women in the brothel but he could not push the envelope any further than that.

The oldest woman among the standing prostitutes wore a yellow sari tied very low exposing her blubbery belly. Some girls stood giggling while others remained indifferent, Tiwari a veteran of most brothels of Grant road felt incongruous and in an unsettled glance at Asif asked him to select any girl. Asif scanned the room and rested his eyes upon a girl wearing blue denim skirts and a white T-Shirt.

Now all the eyes were upon Tiwari and he had to choose a girl.

He reclined on the sofa, squinted at the women and pretending to be impervious and unimpressed said, "Ah! I don't like any of them."

Asif was impressed by his show of adroitness and gawked at his effrontery, with empty pockets he had deftly rejected all the women in the room in the most audacious manner and more importantly got out of the situation without a blemish.

The women were stunned by his abrasive rejection; few merely smiled in amusement and left the room. Salim Bhai was dismayed by his reaction. The older blubbery belly woman rolled her eyes and remarked, "What does this joker want?! Madhuri Dixit!" She stormed out of the room.

The women had left the room except the blue denim girl chosen by Asif, she held his hands and ushered him towards the massive bedrooms.

Tiwari pretended to ignore the snub by the woman and swaggered his way towards the exit followed by the old pimp and Salim Bhai.

The bedroom was large and clean and consisted of a queen size bed covered with a clean bed sheet. He sat on the bed nervously. The first thing, the girl did after entering the room was turn on the air conditioner. She lifted one part of the mattress and pulled out a packet of an imported colorful condom that had a salacious image of a Caucasian woman on its cover. She went on to remove a single condom from the packet and handed it over to him in a prurient manner. He wondered what would she had felt when she would have witnessed such an image first time ever in her life? He was still thinking about that when he heard a knock on the door. The girl waited for him to respond but he continued sitting on the bed. The girl got up and opened the door. A young lad in his early teens entered the door with brand new blue colored napkin made of cloth in his hands.

The boy smiled at him in the most unctuous manner. The girl spoke, "Give him ten rupees for the napkin".

It took a while for Asif to understand the reason behind the boy's obeisance and he quickly reached for his pocket and removed a number of crumpled currency notes. He tried to find a ten rupee note but it was evasive hence he handed the boy a red twenty rupees note instead. The boy happily pocketed the twenty rupees note and did not bother to return the change. He flashed his gratuitous smile and shook hands with him to not only express his gratitude but to also affirm that now the full twenty rupees belonged to him.

The girl locked the wooden door and joined him on the bed. She observed him through her arched eyebrows for a minute and asked, "First Time?"

Asif shook his head in affirmative. She smiled at him.

He tried to break the ice and said, "Do you want money now?"

The girl shook her head in an ambiguous manner but he felt it was better to pay her first and that may make things easier. He opened his wallet and removed four hundred rupees, added to it another hundred rupees from the money given to him by Tiwari and handed over five hundred Rupees to her.

"You are a handsome boy. Don't you have a girlfriend?"

"I had a girlfriend but she got married," he replied trying to keep up the amiable conversation

"You did not touch her?"

"No," he answered.

The girl gently got closer to him, kissing the nape of his neck got up and pulled her white cotton T-shirt over her shoulders baring her erotic black brassiere and hung it on the metal hook on the wall. She had a whitish complexion but could also be passed on as fair according to Indian standards. The moment she bared her body he noticed that it was fairer than her face and neck.

Just as she was about to unhook her bra he prevented her from doing so. Nonplussed she studied his face for a moment and went on to sit on the bed next to him.

"What happened? Do you have any problem?"

Asif didn't react to her question and instead asked her, "What's your name?"

"My name is Sita," she replied.

"Is that your real name?"

"Does it matter if it's my real name or not? Most people are anyway just interested in my body," she sighed.

Asif once again didn't respond and shot another question

"Where are you from?

"I am from Bangalore."

Hearing about Bangalore got him curious though he was aware that Bangalore is miles away from his native Mangalore and does not share many things in common apart from the common malapropism. However, both the cities belonged to the same state and there was a glimmer of hope that Sita may be sympathetic to Jenny if she would have come across her, hence, without wasting any time he asked her,

"Sita, is there a Mangalorean girl by the name of 'Jenny' in this brothel?"

"I never heard that name," she answered blithely.

"Are you sure? Did you ever meet any girl from Mangalore?"

"Yes, I am sure, there were few girls from Karnataka and I don't recall any girl at present or past from Mangalore in this house but why do you ask?"

"You never came across any such girl? Or maybe they changed her name?" He persisted.

"I have been working in this place for last two years and I have not heard of any one called Jenny and even if they changed her name it's impossible for me to miss a girl from Mangalore, trust me she is not here." asserted Sita veritably.

Downcast with disappointment Asif dropped his shoulders. She tousled his hair, nudging him sniggered and said

"Was she a very luscious girl?"

He remained muted.

"You love her, don't you?"

He kept his gaze on the floor. Sita drew near him in her skirt and black bra; she started to rub her breast against back of his shoulders. In any other situation he would have been tempted towards an attractive girl like her but his mind was too despondent to get affected by any carnal desire. She lay down on the bed, her skin was smooth stretched over a curvaceous body and waited for him to come over her but he did not respond and sat motionless. She got up to sit on the bed and said,

"You don't want to have sex? Ok no problem. What about Frenchie?"

He had never heard that term ever before and had no idea what that meant. He looked towards her in astonishment.

"I hope you know what Frenchie is?" She said emphasizing on the word went on to open her mouth and sucked her thumb moving her tongue in the most lascivious manner.

He understood her allusions, got up from the bed and looked away. Sita was smart enough to understand that he wasn't there for sex. She walked up towards the wall and quickly began wearing her T-shirt.

"Sita, I have information that Jenny is in some brothel in Grant Road but I was misled by one pimp who told me she was here."

"You expected these wretched pimps and procuresses to tell you the truth?" she smacked with a grimace and continued, "They burn us with boiling water if we do not agree to sleep with customers but after we start raking in the money, bastards ask us to tie Rakhi on their hands," she scorned.

"How can I find her?" he pleaded.

She gasped and said, "Finding a girl in Grant road brothels is like finding solitary lice in a dense shock of hair."

He had never heard that kind of proverb before and wondered if it was created by her or a commonly used jargon in the world of prostitutes.

She mulled for a while and said

"Ganesh may help you."

"Ganesh, who?" asked, Asif.

"Ganesh, the same boy who brought the napkin," replied Sita.

"You think he can help me? He is just a kid," he quipped

She laughed, "Don't be misled by his age, that lad knows more about Bombay brothels than the police or CID does, he's been raised running errands and doing odd work for pimps and brothels. He is the right person to help you."

Asif was amazed to hear that and also wondered what a fairly cultured and educated girl like Sita was doing in a brothel but he decided to refrain from asking too much personal information about her.

She watched him mulling and remarked insouciantly, "You are wondering, how on earth I landed up in this hell, isn't it?" A ripple of pain went through her. "Well, all I can say is that it's my destiny but I will not stay here longer," she said, filled with an air of confidence.

He felt there was no reason for him to stay in that room any longer and pile more pain to an already woebegone Sita. He got up and tucked his shirt under his trousers, walked towards the dressing table in the corner of the room and combed his disheveled hair that were tousled by her.

He moved to walk towards the door but before he reached the door Sita quickly reached before him and looking in his eyes planted a kiss on his cheeks. He returned her gesture with a smile full of appreciation and dashed out of the door. He watched Salim Bhai converse in Arabic with two Arab boys in the hallway. He ignored them and quickly moved outside the apartment with his heart full of gratitude to this wonderful girl called Sita.

He disgorged out of the building trying hard to control his anger and maintain his equanimity over Ravi Dadhi's deceit. The restaurant below was shut, he noticed Tiwari smoking cigarette on the footpath across the street, struggling to create smoke rings and failing miserably. He was so engrossed with smoke rings that he did not realize Asif's presence. It was near 3 am and there was every likelihood of police patrol in the streets doing night rounds and high possibility of being interrogated by some inebriated policeman around a tourist red light area.

Asif did not say a word but gave a gentle nudge to Tiwari and scurried past him.

Tiwari abandoned his smoke rings midway and quickly paced his steps to join him.

It was Asif who spoke first,

"*Bhenchod* pimp, lied to us"

"You mean Jenny wasn't there?"

"No. Ravi Dadhi lied to us."

Tiwari gritted his teeth and clenched his fist, "We should have broken his face. I will teach that bastard a lesson."

"It will be impossible and suicidal to venture anywhere near Kennedy bridge again," remarked Asif.

"Forget Kennedy Bridge. The pimp will sure emerge out of his burrow someday," saying Tiwari spat on the ground.

"I spoke to that girl and she suggested we should take the help of a young boy who runs errands at Salim Bhai's brothel."

"Ah! You think it will be of any help?" questioned asked an unconvinced Tiwari.

"I don't know but we have to take a chance and return tomorrow."

Tiwari did not respond to him but continued to fume and swear at Ravi Dadhi, continued repeating, "I should have broken his teeth," over and over again till the time they reached home.

7

They returned the next evening to Colaba and sat drinking tea at Gulf Hotel. The hustle bustle of the brothel would start post nine p.m. and six to eight p.m. was the time when the girls got ready with their make-up and other related activities, that was the time when Ganesh was busiest getting biscuits, tea, medicine, beer and depleting condoms.

Asif finished his fourth cup of tea from a long glass. Tiwari was bored and tried to remove his paper for *Matka* tips but Asif admonished him and he reluctantly pushed the paper back into his back pocket. It was almost one hour since they had been sitting drinking tea in the hotel and waiting for Ganesh to emerge out of the building.

Their patience paid off at twenty minutes past seven in the evening when he saw Ganesh emerge out of the building with a jute shopping bag in his hands. Asif quickly got up and made his way outside the hotel. Tiwari attempted to rise and join him but Asif gestured him to stay where he was.

Ganesh was racing fast towards Pasta lane when Asif accosted him jauntily,

"Hello, Ganesh"

Ganesh looked at him with a smile and appeared more than happy to be addressed by his name.

"Hello Sir, are you coming again today? How was yesterday? Hope you had a good time? I am sure Sita *Didi* gave you good service. I know she is good; everyone wants to fuck her." Asif realized Ganesh was not more than fourteen years of age and much younger than he had imagined.

He did not respond to any of the rapid questions thrown in by the young boy and instead said, "Ganesh, I wish to speak to you. Can we sit down somewhere and perhaps have a cup of tea?"

"Right now, no time for tea sir, but I can join you for Beer later, and are you fucking Sita Didi tonight? We can meet after your fuck."

"Ganesh, I am not going to visit the brothel tonight," said Asif

Ganesh instantly blurted, "Oh you are not visiting tonight? No problem. Ah! I think you like new girl's every time right?" saying he tittered, "No problem, I will take you to Ahmad Mansion that's just walking distance from Gulf building, you will get solid sex, our brothel has rotten stuff," he continued "I will take you to the other place, there are all foreigner women and most customers are Arabs, Africans and Europeans. Good girls, big boobs." He went on to explain sexual details explicitly and in the crudest and acerbic fashion that was very disturbing to hear from a teenage lad. He clearly had developed a precocious demeanor at an early age.

"Alright we will have beer together. What time will you come out?"

There was an instant fission in Ganesh's voice, "I will come down at three a.m. after that full night bang-bang begins.

Meet me at the petrol pump." He dashed toward the Pasta lane shops.

It was still early evening and they had a lot of time to kill. They decided to walk towards Regal cinema and bought tickets for the last show. The movie ended at half past midnight, they ambled towards Gateway of India where a number of mawkish small town tourists stood clicking pictures and watching the sea. To pass time, they loitered around Taj Mahal Hotel Gate. Tiwari ogled at white female tourists and made occasional loud ululating noises at the passing Arab tourist families taking joy rides by the sea side on horse carriages and enjoying their expletives in Arabic.

At around two thirty a.m. they made their way towards the petrol pump. The tangy smell greeted them along the sea side.

They reached the petrol pump around three a.m. Ganesh was already waiting for them.

Asif greeted him, "Hey you are on time; we thought you would be late."

"Oh, actually I left early, not too many customers today," said an exultant Ganesh.

"Let's go and drink" said Ganesh, and led the way towards the Sassoon Docks, exhibiting great exigency.

"It's late, where would we find beer as this hour?" quizzed Asif.

"Oh don't bother just stay with me," spoke the boy with an air of ease.

They kept following the young boy along the seaside which was reeking of the smell of rotten eggs and which only grew stronger as they neared the seaside slums or the fishermen's homes.

The sound of waves crashing on the shore was getting audible, wooden fishing boats rocked rhythmically to the waves.

They reached the point where the land ended and the Arabian Sea began

"Just give me money and I will get the beer. Do you also want *Charas* or *Ganja* to smoke? I can get that too."

Asif answered in negative and gave him money for beer and the boy quickly disappeared in the abyss of slums by the sea side.

They stood braving fierce sea winds and within few minutes Ganesh emerged from the darkness like an apparition with beer bottles inside black polythene bags in his hands that made clunking sound after clashing with each other inside the bag. Ganesh displayed great excitement to drink beer.

He said, "Follow me" and jumped inside the sea water. The water was not more than knee high. He made his way towards a wooden boat that was anchored at some distance from the shore. They quietly followed him; he jumped inside the rocking wooden boat and gave a helping hand for them to follow him.

"Who owns this boat?" quizzed Tiwari trying to adjust his hair that got tossed by the strong wind.

It was the first time they had interacted with each other and in fact Ganesh had been so desperate to drink beer that he had completely ignored Tiwari's presence.

"Oh! Don't bother about the boat. It belongs to *Kaka*. He lives in the slums. We use it as our little floating bar and when he objects we give him a bottle of beer," replied Ganesh as he settled down on the shaky boat. It was not a very large boat but big enough for three people to sit comfortably on its wooden deck.

The sky was clear and the moon kept emerging and hiding behind the wispy clouds and they could see each other's faces very clearly. Ganesh had short hair and a lean body with drooping eyes. He spoke remarkably fast and often stuttered as he spoke. The young lad opened the beer bottles with his teeth and spat the cork into the sea. He did not wait for anyone to say cheers or raise a toast and began drinking greedily from the bottle. He drank half of the bottle in one stretch and gave out a huge grating belch.

Tiwari removed a packet of popcorn that they had bought at regal cinema; Ganesh grabbed the popcorns and devoured some of it. Asif waited for things to settle down but an impatient Ganesh continued to talk.

"Sir you just tell me which brothel you wish to go; I can take you to all the places. I will take you to the right places and for the right price. If you go to them at midnight they are in huge demand and won't settle for anything less but if you visit a brothel at three a.m. the bitches have no choice and will sleep for even a sandwich. You see if they don't get a customer it's their loss. The ones that charge five hundred or thousand rupees will at that time screw with you for hundred rupees or give you a great time just for a bottle of beer."

Tiwari listened to the boy with great interest. The beer had a sedating effect upon the kid, as a result of which he calmed down a bit, he spoke in a manner intended to regale and continued his sexually prurient talk with gross explicit sexual details.

"Ganesh, I want you to find a girl for me..." And even before he could conclude the sentence Ganesh rejoined, "Any girl sir, you tell me they are all there." Asif cut him short.

"I want you to find a girl by the name of Jenny, she is in brothel somewhere in Grant road, I have no idea in which brothel she lives but I want you to trace her for me."

"Why, sir? Is there anything special about the girl?"

Tiwari interjected sharply and rasped in a rather abrasive manner,

"Look here. Just find the girl and take whatever money that you want."

The boy was slightly rattled being snubbed by Tiwari. But Asif quickly intervened to placate the boy as he did not wish to intimidate the kid because his role in the task was pivotal. He gently placed his hands on the boy's shoulders in a reconciliatory fashion.

"Look Ganesh, It's important for me and I will suitably reward you if you do me this favor," saying he opened the second bottle of beer for him.

Ganesh quickly grabbed the beer bottle and began quaffing it.

"Grant Road! Hmm, I know some pimps. I can try." He reached for the popcorn in Tiwari's hands.

Munching the popcorns, he said, "Give me some time, I will do my best, I used to live in Foras road before I joined Salim Bhai."

Tiwari was beginning to feel the effects of beer and was turning his tone aggressive by the moment but Asif stopped him by quickly placing his hands on Tiwari's shoulders and squeezing his collarbone.

Ganesh held the bottle of beer in his right hand and retrieved a small plastic pouch of dry weed from his trousers with his left hand. He did not bother to ask permission and merely grabbed the packet of cigarette that was lying in front on him. Removing a single cigarette, he started to empty its tobacco to mix in with the powdered weed and began preparing a joint zealously.

Tiwari was getting increasingly miffed with the boy's temerity yet stayed calm. Ganesh got up to light a lantern and burning it he began cleaning the crushed weed. Ganesh readied the joint, lit the cigarette and took two deep puffs, inhaling and holding the smoke inside for a long time before he exhaled and in no time the whiff of weed was in the air. Ganesh slouched on his back and offered the cigarette to Asif, he declined but Tiwari was eager to smoke the joint.

The boat was full of marijuana smoke. Asif had been drinking in an abstemious way and not been smoking yet the effect of the exhaled smoke was having its effects on him, making him feel foggy. A stoned Ganesh calmed down after the cigarette. He spoke with his back on the boat and eyes towards the sky,

"*Bhai*, you are a gentleman." The first time I saw you in Sita *Didi's* room. I knew you are not the brothel types. I have grown up in brothels, *Bhai*." Suddenly Ganesh had finally dropped his guard and it was evident from his smooth transition of addressing Asif from '*Sir*' to '*bhai*.'

"I was born in a brothel. I know the inside-out of the trade." Meanwhile Tiwari exhaled the smoke up in the sky and offered the joint back to Ganesh and asked him

"You were born in a brothel?"

"Yes in Foras road. As a small child I only had memories of brothel. Some say my mother was a prostitute." He sighed and paused. "Do you know giving birth to a girl is great moment of celebration in brothels? But boys? Who cares for boys, we are pariahs, outcastes. I have no idea who my mother was. She was probably some prostitute who abandoned me or maybe she is still around but does not wish to acknowledge me. Nobody ever told me the truth, now I am no longer interested either," saying he slurped the last drop from the bottle before throwing it into the sea with a splash.

No one spoke for some time. Tiwari kept smoking joint till the filters burnt his fingers. Asif was getting sleepy and looked at his watch it was five a.m., just one hour to go before the morning sun rays would hit the horizon. Ganesh lay on his back; Tiwari was alert and looked at the boy quizzically and was contemplating asking for another joint but gave it up.

Ganesh slowly got up, raised his head and said,

"Bhai, I will do my best for you. If the girl is in Grant Road I will definitely track her down, you should sleep now," so saying he made his way towards the edge of the boat.

"Where are you going? Stay here," requested Asif.

"No, I will sleep on Kaka's terrace in the slums. Both of you can sleep on the boat," saying this he jumped out of the boat into the water, splashing and spilling the water inside the boat he trudged towards the sea side slums. The boat rocked and continued to oscillate for some time. A stoned Tiwari kept glaring at the lantern for a long time finally they both made their way inside the canopy and fell asleep.

Asif woke up with the chatter of seagulls, he looked at the watch and it was half past eleven in the morning. He stirred Tiwari who was slavering from his mouth.

Asif wasn't sure how useful Ganesh would be in the pursuit of tracing Jenny yet he found certain earnestness in the young boy and somewhere deep inside his heart he had certain degree of optimism about him.

Meanwhile Tiwari was angry and embarrassed over the Ravi Dadhi fiasco and tried doing his bit to help but Tiwari would visit the brothels as a customer and it was highly improbable for pimps or prostitutes to divulge information about another prostitute to a customer. It was a highly secretive and dark world and outsiders seldom got to know the happenings inside the secret underbelly.

One could be visiting a brothel and prostitutes for years. The women belonged to various backgrounds, most were forced into the flesh trade others were inveigled by professional procuress women who scouted for prurient girls in rural India and Nepal. Some innocent gullible rural girls were tricked into elopement by promise of marriage by professional pimps who sold them after bringing them into Bombay. Very few had willingly become prostitutes. The pimps could express friendliness, the women may feign all the love for you but that would last only till the time one is within the confines of the brothel. The brothel had varied reactions upon the trafficked girls, some would learn the trick of the trade and quickly start using their body to squeeze out whatever they could, from the men. Some girls would suffer from Pistanthrophobia and resent any gesture or form of affection. Once you step out of the brothels you are out of bounds of oleaginous emotions, bonds and vibes that may have been shared or experienced inside. With such kind of unwritten rules and dark etiquettes being practiced, it was not an easy task to get to the bottom of the truth.

It was almost a week since their drinking binge on the boat and Tiwari had already mentioned their escapade at least a dozen times on how much he had enjoyed drinking in the sea and the boat which rocked like a cradle on the sea.

Asif was wary of returning to Colaba too often fully aware that his purpose of entertaining Ganesh was restricted to getting information. On the eighth day he got a message from Babu Bhai's restaurant that someone called Ganesh had phoned and that he would call back again at seven p.m. in the evening.

They reached Babu Bhai's restaurant at seven p.m. and waited patiently however the phone rang only at seven forty-five p.m. It was Ganesh,

"Bhai, I got some information that there was a girl in Jamuna Mansion. It was difficult for me to get further info but I can say with all certainty that there definitely was one Mangalorean girl at Jamuna Mansion."

"Was her name Jenny?"

"Bhai, I cannot confirm that but I got to know that there was certainly one Mangalorean girl in Jamuna Mansion. Bhai, can we meet three days later? I will surely get more information by then and I won't phone you again, just come directly to Colaba."

"Ok Ganesh, I will meet you after three days."

"Yes Bhai, we will have beer and smoke and I got some new maal (stuff)" saying he hung up the phone in a huff.

Three days later, they reached Gulf Hotel building and waited for Ganesh. It was seven p.m., the approximate time when Ganesh would get down to run his errands. They continued waiting patiently for him to emerge from the building but there was no sign of him. After drinking four to five cups of tea from Ideal restaurant and walking back and forth on Haji Niyaz Ahmed Road towards Pasta lane with no avail, there was no sign of Ganesh. It had been almost two hours and as a result Tiwari began losing patience and started to grumble,

"What do you expect from a pimp?"

Asif was annoyed at the derision of Ganesh by Tiwari. He had faith in the boy and found no malice in the kid. He was irked by Tiwari's use of derogatory words like pimp and wanted to upbraid him for his remarks but chose not to react.

"Let's return at two a.m. We may catch him then," Saying Asif decided to move.

They had a lot of time, hence first they decided to make their way towards Marzban restaurant and then watch a movie.

The nearest cinema was Regal but because they had already watched the movie on previous occasion so Asif walked towards Sterling Cinema Fort to watch the last show. Sterling was one of the elitist Cinema Halls of South Bombay and one of the few Cinemas that played English films, catering to a very niche audience. It had a special last show that started at ten forty-five pm called 'Crème de la Crème'.

Tiwari had never watched a movie at Sterling Theater. It was a completely different world for him. He was awestruck by the people who came to watch the film. Crème de la Crème was the name of the show and it was indeed the elitist crème de la crème of South Bombay that turned up for the last show. The theater boasted of newly acquired technology called Dolby Sound which none of the other cinema halls in India possessed at the time.

The crowd consisted of fair tall and beautiful Parsi and Anglo Indian girls wearing western outfits who smelled so good. Tiwari wondered and told Asif, "Where do these nymphs live? Are they really from Bombay?" It was a complete contrast to the other middle class part of the city that they lived in.

The movie ended at half past one a.m. Tiwari still nervously conscious and reeling with huge inferiority complex said, "You should have at least told me we are going to go to Sterling, I would have at least worn better clothes. Look at me, I look like a truck driver." he protested sheepishly.

Colaba was not too far; it was at walking distance and would take just thirty minutes to reach, besides they had some time so they proceeded by foot.

It was two a.m. when they reached Gulf hotel, most hotels and shops had pulled down their shutters. A couple of taxi drivers stood talking under the street lights, an occasional car passed from the streets, few eunuchs went about asking for money from passers-by in a very troublesome manner. They stood patiently glued outside the Gulf building but there wasn't any movement in and out of the building for thirty minutes. It was half fast two a.m. in the morning when a couple of Africans who probably were Sudanese emerged out of the building however there was still no sign of Ganesh.

It was beginning to get frustrating. Asif was resilient but a wary Tiwari's patience gave up and he was the first to speak,

"Why don't we just go up and check?"

Asif immediately rejected the idea. They persisted in waiting for some more time. It was half past three a.m. yet there was no trace of Ganesh.

"I am feeling sleepy and there is no sign of this boy," snapped Tiwari with eyes drooping. Asif also began to ponder if waiting any further would yield any results. Ganesh would have been out by now if he was inside the brothel yet he refused to believe that Ganesh would not be true to his word. There was a certain sincerity in the boy's voice that had convinced him deep inside his heart that Ganesh would not betray him.

"Let's go to slums, perhaps we can find him there," Asif snapped.

Tiwari's eyes were drooping and he walked in somnambulism however the prospect of having beer inside the sea once again got him charged and he followed Asif without much complain.

They reached the seaside slums and were once again hit by the tangy sea odor that filled their nostrils but in some time they got used to it. The boat where they drank on the previous occasion was floating in the sea at the same place. Contrary to the previous evening there was zero movement of wind in the sea and the silence of the night was colossal, the loudest noise was of barking dogs emerging from the slums. There was only one entrance towards the slums and it was pitch dark. Most houses in the locality had their lights switched off but for a flickering tube light on one of the poles. It was total silence. There was not a single soul to be seen but they were faced occasionally by stray dogs that would emerge from nowhere bark and then withdraw back into the alleys.

"Now where do we go?" questioned a miffed Tiwari

"Let's find out *Kaka's* home, the one who got the beer and the place he slept."

There was not a single soul around whom they could ask the address of *Kaka* at that hour and in the dark of the night, to their rescue from a distance they could hear a man humming on a bicycle. They walked towards him and found out that it was a Nepali watchman who perhaps was an inhabitant of the slum returning from work.

Asif asked him if he knew where *Kaka,* the one who owned the boat lived. The Nepali did not speak and instead pointed towards a house which appeared higher than the rest of the houses in that neighborhood before disappearing in the night. Asif looked at the watch it was four a.m. He was in two minds whether he should leave and return in the morning or proceed to knock the door.

Tiwari was already peeved and in no mood to return one more time hence Asif decided to go ahead. They reached the house and knocked old fashioned iron latch outside the door a few times but there was no response. They waited for few more minutes and knocked the iron latch a few more times but there was again no response from inside.. Just when they were about to turn and leave, the door opened with a rasping sound.

An old gaunt man wearing a vest opened the door rubbing his eyes. They were astonished to see that it was the same pimp who had led them to Salim Bhai's brothel. The old man was reeking with alcohol. He continued to rub his eyes and took a while to settle down and spoke haltingly in all his grogginess,

"What do you want?"

"*Kaka*, we are looking for Ganesh. I have some business with him. We were supposed to meet today".

The old man puckered his face and peered at them suspiciously for some time before he spoke.

"What business? Do you sell or smoke drugs?"

Asif got alarmed and quickly spoke,

"Oh! No *Kaka*, you remember us, you took us to Salim Bhai's place the other day?"

Ganesh had promised me to take us to a very good *Adda*, that's it".

The old man recollected them and was pacified by their words but did not react

Asif spoke again "*Kaka*, if you don't mind, can we buy some beer and also see Ganesh?"

The old man dropped his shoulders and with a forlorn sigh said,

"Ganesh died two days ago."

Asif was shocked. For a couple of minutes, the pregnant silence that hung in the air was completely justified.

The old man took a brief pause and resumed to speak with a lot of pain and sadness resonating in his voice, "He was a very good boy with a kind heart and really cared a lot for me. He would drink beer, smoke *charas* and *ganja* but two days ago he returned at night with another boy whom I had never seen before. Ganesh met me before climbing on the terrace to sleep as usual. The foolish boy injected heroin in his body. It was the first time he had tried that drug and had no idea of the amount of dose or the effect of the new drug upon his body. The idiot ended up taking an overdose and died on the terrace. I found his body in the morning. The other boy had just vanished." He took another pause to swallow his saliva and continued,

"I barely managed to cover his funeral expenses," saying the old man looked at them with certain anticipation. Reeling under the shock of the devastating news of Ganesh's death, Asif tried hard to maintain his poise, reached for his pockets and removed a five hundred rupee note and slipped it in the old man's hands before leaving

He turned around and walked out of the slums as the roosters in the slum coops began crowing at the dawn. Stunned Tiwari followed him silently and did not exchange any words.

They walked to reach the Church gate station. The early morning local trains had already begun to ply. They walked inside a Borivali slow local train on platform number two and entered an empty compartment. Asif sat next to the window and Tiwari on his opposite side. The train slowly chugged out of the platform. He looked out of the window and his heart lamented the death of Ganesh. Though he had met him only a couple of times yet he had grown immensely fond of him and found him very genial. He had also placed all his hopes for tracing Jenny upon him.

The train chugged past Marine lines station, it was Tiwari who spoke in a placating manner, and "At least we know its Jamuna Mansion. I have been there on a couple of occasions, and I can take you there." A grieving Asif did not answer him but merely acknowledged him by nodding his head. He wiped his moist eyes which remained glued to the railway tracks as the train clattered past the Charni Road station.

8

Tiwari wasn't convinced if Ganesh's information about Jenny being in Jamuna mansion would be fruitful but Asif had indubitable faith in him and he was convinced that the boy was telling the truth. Asif wanted to check upon Ganesh's information about Mangalorean girl being present in Jamuna Mansion. It was a crucial bit of information and they had to follow it up.

It was eleven thirty at night. Tiwari was desperate for beer so they entered the Railway bar at Grant Road. It was a very dimly lit place where people thronged in plenty. Some were glued to the television that was placed on an elevated platform. They could see the Indian Bollywood actress Tabu dancing to the beats of a movie song on the TV screen. Tiwari ordered some beer. It was so dark that Asif was amazed and wondered how people found their way in and out of the place in such paltry light. The waiter, whose face was barely visible, brought two bottles of 'Sand Piper beer' along with complimentary boiled pea nuts.

They struggled to see each other's faces in the dim light. Tiwari had already finished one bottle and desperately ordered another beer. Asif was still struggling with his first beer and with his mind already numbed declined the waiter's question on a second. The smoke of oblibanum filled the place as the waiters took orders and returned in a flash while the customers kept entering the restaurant. The screech of a rattling table or squeaking of chair was heard as customers hurried out and in. There was hardly any place to breathe.

It was past midnight but the flow of people continued. Asif looked at his watch, it was ten minutes to one a.m. He got up and asked Tiwari to leave. Tiwari was still savoring the boiled peanuts but despite his consternations reluctantly stepped out of the railway bar. They walked into a side alley towards the pavement where a Chinese food cart stood with some plastic stools placed by its side. A few people stood eating food on the footpath. Tiwari ordered some fried rice and they sat on the stools. Most people there appeared to be in an inebriated state. The smoke of industrial cooking oil used by the Nepali cook mixed along with the smoke of marijuana cigarettes exhaled by some of the customers was floating in the air.

Unexpectedly, it began to drizzle and tiny raindrops dripped down their heads. They ate quickly and made their way towards Jamuna Mansion. Tiwari led the way walking briskly and Asif matched strides with him. They took a few turns and after crossing a road reached a quaint old building that apparently was not less than hundred odd years old, it was known as 'Jamuna Mansion', one of the oldest brothels in Bombay. They quickly made their way towards the building. On the passage outside the entrance of the building they noticed at least eight to twelve people, most of them North Indian migrants in droves, stood peeping inside. Asif wondered why the people were standing outside the building and what they would be looking for. But he didn't have time for all those questions at that moment.

Tiwari took the lead and moved forward by climbing the steps leading towards the first floor. Asif felt the same fetid gut stinking, rebarbative stench that he had endured at Kennedy Bridge brothel. The walls leading up by the steps were full of paan, tobacco stains and the occasional waft of alcohol in the air. When they reached the first floor he noticed numerous rooms with large doors and some unattractive plump women standing on the passage looking for customers. The women wore colorful gaudy sarees exposing their midriff with bad make up on their faces. Some of them flashed an importunate smile, others remained indifferent.

Tiwari entered the third room from the left of the stairs followed by Asif. It was a massive room with a very high roof and most of the space in the room was occupied by beds that were covered above with veils that looked like a non-transparent mosquito net. Tiwari walked up to a middle aged woman who sat on a chair next to the window. Two other girls sat talking to each other in another corner of the room. 'Hi Philomena Aunty,' greeted Tiwari. She answered, *"Kya re bhaiya, bahot time baad aya."* (You returned after a long time?) Tiwari did not answer her and merely smiled. Philomena was an old procuress also known as *'Akka'*, or *Gharwali'*, the senior brothel keeper. She set her eyes upon Asif and studied him for a minute.

Asif raced his eyes all over the room. There were at least six beds in the room, all with non-transparent net covering them. Anyone could simply just lift the cloth, enter the bed to have sex and make a quick exit. Tiwari asked Philomena about a certain girl called Rani. Philomena announced in a loud and harsh manner that Rani was no longer in Jamuna Mansion and had gone to her native place. Tiwari wasn't too pleased to hear her reply and his smile turned into grimace when Philomena aunty suggested he choose another girl called 'Gajra'. He was under no obligation and had a choice of either assenting to Gajra or could choose any other girl of his choice but Tiwari decided to have a peek at Gajra and then make his decision.

Gajra entered the room. She was a skinny girl with tobacco stained teeth and flashed her gummy smile. Tiwari appeared to be satisfied with Gajra and instantly began bonding with her. Asif stood near the door in his green shirt and black jeans. Philomena aunty looked towards him and said, "You don't want to fuck?" Asif shook his head in negative. Just then a girl in her early twenties of whitish complexion and curly hair wearing a cream colored nightgown entered the room and set her eyes upon Asif. She slowly walked towards him and put her arms on his shoulders. He felt her right breast touch him and could swear he knew the brand of hair oil she had on. Asif withdrew a step or two backwards avoided looking into her eyes and instead looked down on the floor.

Philomena was startled watching his reaction and observed the development attentively, but his rejection did not go well the girl and she began to abuse him loudly in Marathi, "Bastard, mother fucker, what do you think of yourself?" Seeing the situation turn ugly Tiwari intervened and took Asif in a corner and said "C'mon man, just do it to her. It will be over in minutes." Asif found the place repugnant and nauseating. He could barely breathe and felt disgusted. He shrugged his head and conveyed to Tiwari that he wasn't interested in sex.

The girl now stopped abusing and watched Asif's movements closely. Tiwari ushered Asif towards his bed and made him sit on the vacant bed next to the one he had chosen. Gajra was already inside the net naked and waiting for him to join her. She popped her head out of the net and looked at him flashing her tobacco stained gummy smile. He saw her and beckoned her to get back inside on the bed.

The prostitute in a nightgown now realized that Asif wasn't interested in her and was in no mood to have sex. So she changed her tactics. She walked tantalizingly next to him and began stroking his hair in an attempt to titillate him. Tiwari watched them cautiously. Asif once again felt her body heat and could smell the scent of her talcum powder along with her perspiration drawing revulsion. He wanted to throw up yet at the same time her touch aroused him but his aversion was stronger and overpowering over, losing control to any erotic urges. Philomena watched the situation with interest as he shrugged and moved away from the girl. The moment Asif withdrew the spurned girl once again got into a fit of rage and with a frown on her face angrily stormed out of the room screaming and reviling, "You will come to me one day, you bastard! You will return one day."

Asif continued to gaze on the ground. Tiwari was relieved to see the girl walk out of the room and readily entered the bed covered with the net. All sorts of noises emerged from outside the rooms, obstreperous women abusing drunkard customers, radio playing songs combined with the sounds of grunts and moans of Tiwari and his girl. Their bed started to rock in rhythm to their sex. The iron bed moved with cranking noise and he could see Tiwari's and the girl's legs emerge out of the bed. The bed kept rocking for a while before it suddenly came to an abrupt stop.

Asif expected Tiwari to step out of the net but instead he heard Tiwari's voice from inside the net "Asif, everything ok?"

"Yes I am fine," he rejoined.

The bed started to move once again, the moans of the girl and loud groans of Tiwari could be heard once again, it was very loud and noisy. An indifferent Philomena kept impassively looking outside the window and none of the other women in the room paid any attention either. Asif thought Tiwari was taking unusually longer time as the bed continued to rock and then it came to a grinding halt with a huge grunt from Tiwari.

There was absolute silence for a minute and then he heard the tobacco stained girl say to Tiwari, "How much did you drink?" There was an inaudible and incomprehensible response from inside the net in form of whispers. Tiwari had paid for an hour but he had sex only once and he spent rest of the time talking with the girl inside the net.

After sometime Tiwari emerged out of the net followed by the giggling Gajra. Tiwari looked at him and winked nodding affirmatively, which was a positive sign. He dashed out of the room followed by Asif. It was late night but customers still kept trickling in. Jamuna Mansion was the cheapest brothel of Bombay and the majority of the customers were poor migrant workers from other states. The charge for a short time sex was a mere fifty rupees. They reached outside the building and could see more men waiting outside the entrance of the building. Asif asked, "Tiwari, who are those people standing outside?" Tiwari sneered and answered, "They are all impecunious, *'Phookat Chodoo's'* or 'Free fuckers'. These people have no money for sex, *saale,* are expecting some acquaintance to pay for them!" he chuckled.

They arrived at the main road, Asif was desperate to know the results of Tiwari's conversation with Gajra and impatiently asked him what she had revealed. Tiwari lit a cigarette and said, "Gajra says there was a Mangalorean girl in Jamuna Mansion but she has been moved to another brothel. She is unaware where she has been moved but she says Philomena knows the location." Asif was relieved to hear the news. It was a good lead but he would now have to deal with Philomena and cracking her was not an easy task. She was Akka or the head procuress of the brothel and had been in the business for many years. Nevertheless, he realized it was good news and they were getting closer to finding Jenny and at the moment the best option available was Philomena.

Tiwari was still unsure and said, "Why would she reveal the truth? She is an old hat in the business and, not the one to be swayed by anything. She lives off other young girls. The young new prostitute recruits are valuable commodities for her. She isn't a pliable woman and will not divulge anything about Jenny even if she knows it and moreover the first thing these people do in brothel with new girls is that they rechristen the new bride as they call them and give them new names. I wonder if they would even know Jenny by her original name."

"I will try! I will try my best," muttered Asif. Tiwari wasn't too optimistic, yet he affirmed his support by nodding his head. They planned to go to Jamuna Mansion again and there was no guarantee that Philomena would know if Jenny was in Jamuna Mansion at all.

Asif was convinced that there weren't many prostitutes from Mangalore in Bombay and if at all Jenny had come across Philomena, she would have surely known her.

The next evening Asif was busy with the India versus Sri Lanka cricket match. It was a day and night match and he got free only at half past eleven. He met Tiwari at midnight. Tiwari was reeking with alcohol. Asif gave him a disapproving look but embarrassed Tiwari mawkishly said, "I just had a couple of pegs." Asif did not believe him but he was in no mood to sermon him either.

They started to walk and caught a taxi at New Shireen theatre that took them to Grant Road. They stopped the taxi near Khareghat Parsi colony. It was a housing colony for lower middle class members of the Zoroastrian *Parsi* community. Tiwari walked towards the paanwala to buy his packet of *gutka*, while Asif stood on the road leading to Khareghat colony. From one of the allies inside the colony emerged Hoshang, their old acquaintance and he looked at Asif and blustered in his usual Parsi jocular manner, "*Gandu Sala!* What are you doing here?"

Hoshang was not a very huge man but in contrast to his physique he had a very blusterous and towering voice. Asif smiled and responded, "Hello Hoshang, I am here with Tiwari." A visibly tipsy Hoshang looked at Tiwari and bawled, "Hey mother fucker Bhaiya, what are you doing here?" Asif was peeved at rambunctious Hoshang but he knew Hoshang was an irritant and snubbing him would only add fuel to fire and chose not to respond to his antics.

An impish Tiwari was tickled to see Hoshang and responded blithely in his usual banter, "*Bawa!* Do you stay here?" Hoshang replied, "Mother fucker, yes I stay here. What the fuck are you doing here?" Tiwari enjoyed provoking him and went on teasing Hoshang who in response kept haranguing in his loud and raucous voice. Asif was increasingly losing patience with Hoshang and wanted to leave. He looked towards Tiwari and signaled him to leave. Tiwari in response looked towards Hoshang and said, "Hoshang, we are coming to your home. Won't you invite us for dinner, introduce us to your beautiful wife and treat us with some *Dhansak?*"

This got Hoshang into a rage and he blasted loudly "Mother fucker, I will never let you step into my home, not even on my funeral," saying this he quickly turned and started to stagger back inside the colony. Tiwari laughed loudly and Asif in spite of the trauma could not help but smile.

They reached Jamuna Mansion where some '*phookat chodoo's*' thronged outside the entrance as usual. They entered the building and started climbing the wooden steps, familiar wave of malodorous redolence hit Asif's senses drawing his revulsion. It was his second time and he was acquainted with the building.

They entered Philomena's chamber. A bald middle aged man stood talking with Gajra, the skinny girl with whom Tiwari had sex with the previous night. The moment she saw him she immediately pushed the ostensibly drunken bald customer and rushed towards Tiwari who opened his arms looking into her eyes in a very filmy manner.

The drunken bald customer balanced himself and stood near the steps watching them. He moved to leave but suddenly turned around and abused the girl, *'Saali Chinal'*. An enraged Tiwari lunged forward in the man's direction to hit him but Asif swiftly restrained him and pulled him back. The drunkard hobbled his way out grumbling and abusing.

It took less than a minute for Tiwari to calm down. They entered Philomena's chamber and Tiwari settled down on the bed with the girl snuggling up to him. Philomena who sat near the window opened a gutka packet and started to chew it. She didn't speak but kept looking at a rather languid Asif. Tiwari was just about ready to enter the partitioned net bed when the girl who Asif had snubbed the previous night entered the room wearing the same cream colored nightgown with half a smile on her face, "I knew this *chikna* would return." So saying she sat on the bed beside Asif. He involuntarily looked at her and she smiled at him in return and placed her hand near his crotch and stimulated her fingers. He felt blood rushing through his veins arousing his sexual desire yet he also felt an abominable aversion towards her. The revulsion towards this girl and the loathsome place was far greater than any bit of amorous feelings infused by her touch.

The smell of her cheap perfume mingled with hair oil along with sweat wafted across towards him. She slipped her hands further towards his crotch but he resisted her probing hands and pushed her hand away. She was outraged on being snubbed and exploded, "Mother fucker, what do you think of yourself?"

She was about to hit him but stopped when she noticed Tiwari rising to stand on guard and withdrew. Asif glanced towards Tiwari who responded by keeping his finger on his lips suggesting him not to respond to the girl's malevolence or expletives.

The pugnacious girl continued to abuse in Hindi then switched to Marathi and again back to Hindi. Almost gloating in choicest abuses she also added some standard English abuses in her vituperations. *Kutra, Haramkhor,* Nonsense, Bastard, *Haramazada,* Nonsense. Asif remained mum and didn't respond to her provocations. Philomena who was watching all along intently, out of the blue intervened and blurted, *"Randi Saali,* he does not want to sleep with you, get lost!" The girl's abusive tirade suddenly ended in a whimper. She was left rattled by Philomena's intervention and giving a rather wry look left the room in a huff.

Asif walked towards Philomena and sat near her. She in turn was surprised to watch him approach her and that instantly resulted in a change in her demeanor. She was no longer the rude Akka but transformed into a coy woman. She smiled at Asif and glanced at Tiwari who smiled back

"Aunty, this Asif is a native of your Mangalore," Philomena was impressed upon hearing that but she was not a credulous person and immediately started to speak in Tulu the local language of the Mangalore district.

"*Oordar?*: she asked Asif with a smile. *'Oordar'* a common term in Tulu language that referred to a person from same village or which literally translates as 'My villager'

Asif smiled and replied in Tulu, *"Danay Oordar"*, which meant "Yes, Native Villager." Before she could ask him further questions in Tulu he confessed that he knew nothing more than a smattering Tulu since he was born in Bombay, yet Philomena was already excited and asked him which part of Mangalore he belonged to. Asif answered, "Moodbidri!" Philomena flashed a generous smile and quickly added, "I am from 'Malpe'."

It was a coastal town known to him. Asif acknowledged and said "Yes I know 'Malpe.' It has a beautiful beach." That brought another big smile on her face.

Philomena aunty in her fifties with a belly had an attractive face. She wore an orange saree and with her age she no longer appeared like a very luscious woman yet when she saw Asif drawn towards her it brought out the woman inside her. She marveled at him while adjusting her blouse and was clearly mesmerized by the fact that he had displayed interest towards her.

"Madam, I think my friend is in love with you," interjected Tiwari in a rather silly manner. Philomena was bedazzled to hear these words but shot back rather bluntly, "Shut up bastard. Don't teach me about love in a brothel. It remains as long as the erection lasts." As a result of being snubbed Tiwari quickly withdrew and slipped inside the net bed with the gummy girl.

Asif continued where Tiwari had left, "I wish to sit with you," and saying he prepositioned Philomena using the brothel language that meant he wished to have sex with her. Philomena was amazed hearing upon his desire. She smiled and looked towards the wall clock. It was one thirty a.m. She said to him, "Do you want to sit for a short time?" In plain terms that meant to have sex for not more than thirty minutes approximately.

Asif replied, "No."

She looked towards him again and asked, "Long time?" That meant one hour.

Asif again replied in negative.

Bemused she looked into his eyes and asked, "So, what do you want?"

"Full Night." was his answer.

Philomena could not believe her ears. It had been ages since she had been asked by any customer for a full night service

She was astonished by the fact that most men would often chose nubile young girls and the young handsome boy wanted to bed her for 'Full Night' She spat the tobacco from her mouth that she was chewing on the corner of the walls and once again looked at the wall clock and said, "You will have to wait for another half an hour." Asif nodded in the affirmative.

Meanwhile, Tiwari had been grunting loudly in their current session inside the net on the bed and the iron bed rocked noisily for a while before it came to a grinding halt like a local train slowly chugging on a railway platform.

Asif waited for Tiwari to get out of the bed. He was peeved that Tiwari was taking unusually longer to get out of the bed in spite of getting over with his sexual act. He looked towards the wall clock. It was forty-five minutes past one and another fifteen minutes to go before two am. Tiwari languorously dragged himself out of the bed. Asif went up to him and informed him that he was going to spend entire night with Philomena. Tiwari crinkled his nose in amazement to the fact that Asif had managed to pull a coup. Tiwari took a deep breath and asked "How much did u fix it for?" Asif had no answer because he had not negotiated the deal with her and perhaps Philomena too was so overwhelmed with his offer that she had also not bothered to quote or demand a price.

Tiwari smiled wryly and asked "Do you have money for full night with you?" Asif nodded assuring him that he did.

"Okay. All the best! I will go home now. See you in the morning," Tiwari winked and amiably patted Asif on the back, before he left.

A couple of young girls entered the room and stood talking in one corner of the room, Philomena got up and said, "Stay here, I will be back," before leaving the room. The two other girls present in the room giggled and tittered behind their hands. He understood their innuendo; they were ridiculing him for having sex with the much older Philomena instead of them but he ignored them and maintained his attention at the clock.

There was no sign of Philomena for forty minutes and it was almost fifteen past two. His impatience was growing by the second. Suddenly Philomena walked in wearing a pink nightgown, her hair flowing and still wet with the shower. She walked towards Asif and said "I am going to charge you five hundred rupees for the night."

Asif nodded perfunctorily in agreement. She nudged his arms and pointed towards the adjacent room. He followed her quietly, he had not seen this room before and realized that it was a much better room. He noticed three to four other smaller cubicle rooms within the room that were separated by wooden partition made of plywood.

Philomena attempting her seductive best led him towards the last room. All the other rooms it seemed were occupied. After Asif entered the room she closed the door. He lay on the bed with his clothes on. His eyes were on the rotating ceiling fan overhead. It was a very old fan that revolved with a sound which went *gung, gung* but it gave much needed relief from the sweltering humidity.

All forms of different noises could be heard from the adjacent partitioned compartments. Sometimes he could hear a leg kicking the wooden plywood other times a jingle of bangles, rapid moans or bed squeaks. Philomena lay on the bed by his side, her hair still wet from the shower. He could also feel the scent of the soap that she had used in the shower.

She looked towards Asif and asked, "Aren't you going to undress?"

He did not respond. She laughed playfully, "Ha ha! Shy lad" and attempted to lift her pink nightgown over her head but Asif stopped her and said, "Not now." She was a bit piqued and not able to surmise his actions. She was an obtrusive woman yet surprisingly remained calm and did not react. She lay on the bed next to him and began stroking his hair. "When did you join this trade?" he asked in a bid to break the ice and get the conversation started. He knew it would not be easy to get her talking unless she felt at ease with him. She did not respond and continued stroking his hair. He tried one more time addressing her by her name, "Philomena, when did you join this trade?" She gazed at the ceiling and slowly withdrew her hands. There was a silence of a couple of minutes before she spoke in solemn tone "I was abducted by a man." Asif turned towards her, his body touching hers and he could feel the warmth of her body. He lay on the left side and supported his head with his left arm as he asked, "Abducted?" She remained glued to the ceiling for a long time before she spoke again.

"One rascal from Mangalore abducted me. I was returning from school. He lifted me and pushed me in the back of his truck," no emotions reflected in her eyes but her sullen rue remained evident.

Asif did not prod any further on the identity of the abductor but instead asked her, "Did you ever go back to your village?"

She looked straight into his eyes and answered scornfully. "Go back? I had two younger sisters. Who would have married them? How could they face the ignominy of having a blemished prostitute elder sister? That would have meant a death knell for them and my entire family."

Asif wanted to keep talking yet at the same time he did not wish to press on her too hard or antagonize her either. There was a moment of silence amidst carnal noises continuing from the adjoining rooms.

Philomena lay next to him as her hands travelled his body and reached around his pelvic region. He did not react but her touch resulted in blood rushing through his veins. She understood that he had got an erection and she began unbuttoning his shirt with great dexterity. A huge wave of sexual temptation swept through him, yet at the same time he was adamant to hold on to his irrevocable aim to find Jenny and not indulge in sex. She unzipped his jeans and touched his manhood with both hands and attempted sliding lower to go down but he stopped her from doing so. She looked at Asif in an imperious way and could not understand what he was looking for. She attempted to go down one more time but was again stopped by him. She glared towards him for a few seconds and then her smile turned into a frown. Frustratingly she stared at him searchingly for a while trying to understand him. She abruptly conjectured something in her mind and exploded in a paroxysm of anger, "Bastard, what are you here for? Tell me?" Asif was fazed but remained muted.

"Give me the money," she demanded.

He immediately reached for his wallet and paid her. His obeisance had a mollifying effect on her but she had not completely gotten over her convulsion of anger and turned her body towards the other side of the bed and feigned sleep.

He lay awake with his eyes open but did not have the courage to start another conversation with her after her outburst and lay speechless in the position for a long time. He did not wear a watch but thought it would be at least four a.m. in the morning by now. An invisible mosquito whined inside the room. The voices had ceased to emerge from the adjoining cubicle rooms and he was also beginning to feel drowsy and felt helpless as he could do little besides lying on the bed. Then to his utter surprise Philomena suddenly turned her face towards him.

She began stroking his hair and spoke in a benign tone, "Why have you come to me? Tell me the truth, what are you expecting from me?" He knew his moment had arrived. He looked towards her and in a childlike innocence spoke "Philomena, I am looking for a girl." She looked into his eyes admiring his candor and asked, "Which girl? And how do you imagine I would know her?"

Asif looked into her eyes and said, "She's from Mangalore and her name is Jenny." There was an apparent change in her countenance.

"Why are you searching for her?" She asked

"I love her," he answered.

Philomena's attitude changed drastically. She was no longer the obstinate rude woman. She adjusted herself on the bed, her hands were still stroking his hair but it was not of a wanton woman but a motherly caress.

"What will you do after meeting this girl?" she asked. Asif's heart fluttered hearing those words and his inner voice resonated that Philomena knew Jenny.

He replied, "I don't know. I just know that I love her and want to see her," She noticed tears glistening in his eyes and kept mulling for a while, licked her lips before allowing the veils of secrecy to fall.

She spoke with a sigh, "Jenny! What a lovely girl." An unfortunate victim of fate she was here sometime back but now has been moved to A-one brothel at Pavalla Street. Don't ever let it out that I have leaked this information to you or else all the other *gharwalis* and pimps will be after my life." She got up wore her nightgown kissed his forehead and walked out of the room.

9

The moment Tiwari heard about A-one brothel it brought at smile upon his face. "Hmmm! Bombay A-one? I know the place," he said with a mischievous smile. "I have an item there," he tittered with a sly twinkle in his eyes. "It's been a while since I have been there but it shouldn't be a problem getting in that place or locating Jenny if she is indeed there."

His words gave hope to Asif. "You think it will be possible to get her out of that hole?" Tiwari ceased to smile and said, "That will be impossible. It's a very heavily fortified brothel, full of pimps and their cronies"

"Should we report it to the police?" asked Asif. Tiwari scoffed, "The pimps pay regular *hafta* (bribe) to the local police station and are well protected by them, nothing is going to come out of it."

"What if we report to the senior police?" Asif persisted not willing to give up.

Tiwari scorned, "You think these local police allow the flesh trade and trafficking of so many young girls without the connivance of senior police officials? They are all hand in glove and part of the chain. The seniors also get a cut of *hafta*." Some may not be directly involved but even if we manage to get them to raid the place there will be enough moles among the police to tip off the pimps. Most young birds will be flown from the coop and the old retired whores will be left for display." Tiwari licked his lips and said "First let's locate her and then we can think of the next step."

Grant Road was a huge bustling place it was not too far from Mahalaxmi Railway Station. On the western railway line after Mahalaxmi and Bombay Central, Grant Road was the next station. Asif didn't wish to waste any time and wanted to set off for A-one immediately but Tiwari advised him against it and instead suggested to be strategic and visit in the evening when most prostitutes would be available. Unlike other brothels, A-one was located on the busiest streets of Grant Road yet incredible as it may seem the locals coexisted and turned a blind eye to the active brothel in their midst. One could easily pass unnoticed under a brothel. Life went on as normal on the main street with the traffic, purveyors and shoppers moving along rubbing shoulders with each other and yet overtly oblivious or perhaps blinkered to the bustling flesh trade in the vicinity. The pavement outside the building was full of hawkers selling various items like electronic goods, books, old debonair magazines and foreign brand condoms displaying images of luscious nude Caucasian women on its cover. The shoppers consisted of both men and women. The women would buy items from hawkers and turn a blind eye to the raunchy condoms on display and they would instead bargain and buy their desired stuff.

After emerging out of the Grant Road station, Tiwari walked ahead on the busy road towards Lamington Road. Asif followed his trail walking briskly through the crowd of shoppers. Tiwari suddenly took a left turn into a dark alley that led inside a building. Few hawkers stood selling hosiery in the alley but were hard to notice in the alley because of the dim light. Asif momentarily lost sight of Tiwari only to find him again when he accidently bumped into him.

Tiwari spoke in hushed voice and asked him to follow him. He swerved towards the right side on the staircase leading up. The iron staircases in spite of being very old and archaic were in remarkable working condition. He reached the first floor and found the place extremely dark and gloomy and an abominable reeking fetid redolence filled his senses, a similar vile stench that marked the other brothels but it was only worse at A-one because there was barely any ventilation. Some girls stood under the dim light bulb but Tiwari did not stop at the first floor and raced up on the steps towards the second floor. Asif wondered why Tiwari did not bother to check the first floor, Jenny could be in any room yet he did not ask any questions and calmly followed him.

Unlike the first floor, no girls stood on the passage of the second floor, instead a young man in white shirt stood speaking to another older man. Tiwari waved at the young man in white shirt who waved back at him. Tiwari entered the open room nearest to the staircase, and Asif followed him meekly. It was a clean and tidy room devoid of any furniture but instead a parallel wooden platform was in place for people to sit. It also had a wooden telephone stand in the corner. Tiwari ushered him to sit on the wooden platform and went on to enter the door leading inside, towards the other rooms.

Asif sat alone in the newly painted room. He looked around and saw few pictures of Gods in frames hung on the walls with red bulbs below the glass frame that illuminated in the shape of a lamp. The smoke of sandalwood flavored incense sticks combined with the stench of brothel filled his nostrils.

He discerned that A-one was certainly a better place than Jamuna Mansion or Kennedy Bridge. The prostitutes often emerged from the rooms, peeped at him and went back. He waited patiently for Tiwari to return. Tiwari tried searching for Sapna his favorite girl in A-one house, the one according to him who pretentiously claimed to love him. He had been having sex with her for a long time and shared some degree of bonding but changed his mind and made a deal with a short girl with curly hair, they emerged outside the inner section followed by an older woman in her thirties. The older woman, apparently a procuress looked at Asif and asked him in an imperious manner if he wanted to have sex. Tiwari promptly answered on his behalf, "*Akka,* He will do it after some time. First let me go with my darling." saying he placed his arms around the curly hair girl. The old procuress walked outside and stood chatting with the men meanwhile Tiwari asked the curly hair girl to go inside the room. Tiwari whispered to Asif, "I will be back soon." He disappeared into the door leading inside.

Asif looked at the wall clock placed next to the frame of Sai Baba. The clock struck eight. All sorts of men entered and exited the brothel. The vigilant procuress stood speaking to the two men and in some time two other men joined them. As time went by the place got busier and noisier by the minute. The sandalwood flavored *Agarbatti* had extinguished yet the smoke pervaded the air. He did nothing but patiently wait for Tiwari to come out.

More men entered and left the rooms after having sex. Some of the men would come out accompanied by the prostitutes they had sex with and would stand outside to speak for a while under the watchful eyes of the procuress and pimps. After the customers left most of the times the women would giggle and make fun of the customers behind their backs, others would immediately rush back inside to be ready for the next customer.

Asif got increasingly restless but in the meantime, Sapna the girl Tiwari regularly had sex with got a wind of Tiwari's presence and was miffed when she found out that Tiwari had chosen to have sex with the curly hair girl over her. When she caught him emerge out of the room she confronted him and accused him of breaching her trust. He shot back at her, "How can you stop me from having sex with other women when you sleep with hundreds of men night and day?" Sapna answered "I do it for my survival. I don't have a choice but you do." Tiwari was left speechless. Sapna was disheartened to see him have sex with the another girl and stormed outside with a disapproving look on her face. Tiwari followed her and stood speaking to her outside for a few minutes and returned. He adjusted himself on the wooden platform next to Asif and lit a cigarette.

The old procuress and the men sat parallel outside the main door. The pimp in the white shirt entered the room with a bottle of beer in his hands. The procuress had a vigilant eye focused inside as well as outside the door. Tiwari waited for the opportunity to speak when they were alone for a few minutes. The moment second white shirt pimp entered the other door. Tiwari grabbed the opportunity and quickly spoke, "I spoke to Sapna, there's a Mangalorean girl. She's known as Tara. I will speak to Akka and if she asks you any questions just say you want to sleep with Tara. Ok?"

Asif was not satisfied with the little information and wished to ask more questions but was edgy about talking louder or asking too many questions. Tiwari got up and proceeded to speak to Akka outside the main door. After exchanging few words, he hurriedly returned, "I spoke to Akka, Tara is in room number five. You have a deal for a short time sex. It's one hundred and twenty-five rupees, but just keep one thing in mind, incase it's the wrong girl you pay her the money whether or not you have sex. We have already waited here for too long so let's not waste any more time, get inside the room immediately. I will be waiting at Shabnam hotel near Apsara Theater." Asif nodded his head in acquiescence and asked where room number five was located.

"Just walk in straight. It's the fifth room to the left," he cut short further instructions seeing Akka approach.

Akka spat the *gutka* in her mouth and addressed Asif in a very coarse manner "Hey get inside. The girl is ready." She turned and walked back towards the main door. Tiwari made a hasty exit and Asif nervously made his way inside, towards the fifth room.

Asif waited outside the fifth room. The partition door opened. A Sikh man with a red turban and khaki shirt who apparently appeared like a taxi driver sat on the bed wearing his socks. Asif tried to locate Jenny but she was not visible. The Sikh wore his shoes and left the room. A pimp stood outside the door. Asif was about to enter the room when a voice implored from inside, "Don't send any more clients." He hesitated and stopped at the door. Through the half open door, he could see a girl in a brown nightgown lying on the bed facing the plywood partitioning the other room.

The pimp standing outside noticed a reluctant Asif and shouted back at the girl inside "Tara, don't act smart. Just shut up and do your job."

Asif slowly entered the dark hideous room. He noticed a dirty malodorous bed sheet covering the bed that had all sorts of stains on it like tobacco; beetle juice or even dried semen. Some used paper napkins littered the floor. After entering the room, he gently sat on the bed. The motionless girl was completely emaciated, enervated and lying on the bed with her head facing the sunmica plywood partition wall.

He pushed himself further on the cot and realized that it wobbled with a grating sound; he adjusted his position and stayed immobile waiting for the girl to react. After a deadlock of five minutes the girl managed to drag herself to sit on the bed with her back resting on the partition but her face was still not visible and completely covered by her long hair. She turned her face towards him and pushed back her long hair that covered her face.

Asif recognized Jenny. She was a pale shadow of the girl he was besotted with and was part of his memories. She looked much older than her age; her lips had turned black and dark crow feet under her eyes. She raised her head and turned her face in his direction but did not look into his eyes. Those lovely blue angelic eyes that bewitched him now reflected a gloomy visage.

He was speechless and peered at her with tears glittering in his eyes. Jenny had not bothered to look at him and went on to cursorily pull her night gown over her head; her body was completely bare devoid of any under garments. She lay on the bed naked and waited for the new customer to satisfy his lust upon her. He was thunderstruck, tears streamed from his eyes and she lay motionless and muttered, "C'mon, just finish it fast. I am not well. I have fever", she spoke impassively in the most uncouth manner. The girl who once could not speak proper Hindi now spoke in the most guttural Bombay accent.

Asif gathered himself and uttered only one word, "Jenny."

Jenny was jolted to hear her name and slowly sat up. It had been a long time since anyone had addressed her with her real name. She was now, 'Tara'.

She turned her face towards him and stared at him for a long time. It was a very somber moment. No questions were asked nor answers given.

Asif began crying loudly. Jenny slowly crawled from the bed towards him and covered his mouth with her hands to deaden his sobs and make sure that pimps did not hear his wails. She went on to feel his entire face with her feeble fingers, his eyes, his nose, cheeks. She did not say a word but her countenance was stamped with a mingled melancholy that rendered it painful to contemplate.

She continued to caress his face for a long time, completely oblivious to the fact that she stood stark naked. She hugged him and pulled him towards her burying his head on her shoulders. His tears continued to drop over her shoulders that were soon completely wet with his tears.

She retrieved a tissue paper under the mattress and wiped his tears. Asif spoke in English trying hard to stifle his sobs, "What happened, Jenny?"

She answered in Bombay accented Hindi, "*Sab Khallas*. It's all over."

There were no emotions or tears in her eyes. He tried hard to control his tears but more drops crashed through his eyes. She wiped his tears as she spoke, "Asif, all my tears have ceased and dried up. I have wept day and night. There are no more tears left in my eyes."

Asif gathered himself and kissed her forehead and he could instantly feel that her body was burning with fever, "Jenny, you are not well!" She shrugged her head and said, "Who cares? Does it matter if I live or die? I am just an object. I don't wish to live either. It's better that I die and end this misery."

"Jenny how did you reach this place?" Her eyes remained glued to the floor for a while then she looked into his eyes and said, "Asif, I missed you a lot, ever since you left that day, I was never the same. I felt terrible for spurning your love and realized how much I had loved you. I missed you, night and day all those years and when I finished college, I knew I could not wait any longer. I had to meet you but I did not know how to contact you. My classmate Padma's uncle Sudhakar who lived in Bombay was visiting the village in those days. I had confided to him about my desire to visit Bombay and he said he would help me meet you as he knew about your family in Bombay.

I was so much in love, innocent, naïve, blind and I did not imagine this city would be so cruel and remorseless. There were no emotions as she spoke, "I left home without telling my father, I left from Udupi Station with Sudhakar Shetty. He was a fifty-year-old man with two children. I trusted him. He had a daughter of my age. He used to address me as *Mugaal* (child in Tulu).

We reached Dadar station the next morning. He took me to his flat in Sion Koliwada. When I entered the flat it was empty. I asked him about his family. He told me they had all gone to Shirdi pilgrimage and would return by evening. He left for work and said that he would return in the evening along with his wife and children.

I was apprehensive but also excited by the thought of meeting you soon. I watched TV the entire day. The day went by and it was evening and then night fell. I waited for him to come but nobody came. I was afraid, completely alone in the house but kept waiting for Sudhakar's family. It was late night and I was hungry I searched the kitchen and ate some biscuits that I found.

I kept my eyes on the door and waited for the door to open. Around two a.m. there was a knock at the door. I nervously rushed to open the door, it was Sudhakar. I was shocked and petrified. I asked him where his wife and daughters were. He did not answer me and locked the door from inside. I could smell alcohol, he was drunk. I was scared and tried to talk to him but he would not answer any of my questions, instead he dragged me into the bedroom and forced himself upon me. I kept crying and pleading all night. I kept screaming as he ravaged me. My virginity was my most precious gift that I had preserved for you and got defiled. He was an animal, my cries and my shrieks gave him more thrill. He kept plundering me the whole night.

The morning brought only grief but also physical pain to my life. I tried to scream and tried to run out of the door but I could barely move. I was in so much pain but that did not stop me from fighting back but the bastard gagged me and tied me to the chair. He did not even let me speak and wanted to rape me again and started to beat me in an attempt to silence me and when that did not work he mixed something in my drink and I passed out.

When I woke up I was in a brothel, some of the pimps here are known to him. Sudhakar knew I would never return to Mangalore again and there was no one who could help me in Bombay. I had never left our little village my entire life and now I was in this unknown brothel of this strange city full of drug addicts and alcoholics.

At first the pimps and *Akka* tried to force me to have sex with a bald old man who had paid a hefty amount for me. I screamed and ran and fought him every time he entered my room. In the end the pimps and *Akkas* pinned me to the bed held my hands as the despicable old man forced himself upon me. I screamed and cursed but he had no mercy upon me. That was just the beginning of my ordeal each day. I was forced to have sex with different and sometimes multiple men, strange men that stink abominably from their bodies and their mouths, that have skin diseases and revolting habits that were unheard and unknown to me. Soon my resistance was broken and I had no choice but to surrender. I pretended to confer to their rules and managed to reach a telephone booth and informed my father but in the middle of my conversation the savages pulled me back towards this hell. I am not allowed to leave the brothel. All of these pimps are the informers of Sudhakar Shetty. The bastard has such a respectable image of a family man in Mangalore but no one knows he has an evil empire in Bombay."

It was very painful for Asif to listen to her trauma but he had to endure it and listen to the truth. He was full of rising torrents of rage, his blood boiled listening to Jenny's excruciating saga. He wiped his tears and held her by his chest and said, "Jenny, I will get you out of this place. We will go back to Mangalore." "I do not wish to return to Mangalore," she retorted. "Alright, we will not go back to Mangalore but I will get you out of this hell". She did not respond or show any exuberance or elation and just remained muted like a ghost.

Someone banged the door, "Come out, are you done with your act? Your time is up?" It was the in-house *Akka* screeching in her exasperating voice. Asif was infuriated and wished to go out and hold the people by their throat smash their heads to pulp and draw blood but better sense prevailed, he knew if he would take any impulsive decision or create trouble, that would be detrimental to Jenny's safety.

He looked into Jenny's eyes and tried to assure her, "I will return soon. Don't worry Jenny. I will get you out of this place." A brooding Jenny wearily pushed her hair out of her eyes, did not respond and maintained a stoic visage. It was a very painful moment for him to leave her in that situation, full of burning fever to be again ravaged by other men.

He walked out of the door and noticed the white shirt pimp sat drinking beer on the passage he walked straight to him and said, "The girl is not well, she has fever and not in a position to give any good service." 'Service' in brothel jargon meant giving a good time in the bed.

The pimp was enjoying his beer and dry peanuts and did not like being distracted from his revelry. He called the procuress, "*Akka,* Tara is doing some drama have a look at *saali.* She is not well, why are you sending customers to her?" An agitated and sullen *Akka* grumblingly walked in from the hall and stood in facing Asif, "Did the bitch throw any tantrums?" Asif implored "No *Akka,* she really has very high fever." It had a bit of calming effect upon her and she walked inside Jenny's room. He could hear *Akka* address her curtly as she entered the room, "Are you not well?" There was no answer from Jenny. She asked her one more time "Are you not well?" Jenny did not respond. *Akka* stormed out of the room and yelled to the other girls curtly "Take the whore on the top. We have this house to run. It's not a hospital to cure sick people" Asif didn't move and stayed near the pimp silently waiting and watching the situation.

Two girls entered the room and emerged out of it holding Jenny by her hands. They walked past Asif; Jenny did not raise her head and was oblivious to his presence. They walked slowly towards the last room leading towards an iron ladder that elevated towards an attic. Asif looked up It was dark and dingy; there were no lights up there. He watched with grief as Jenny struggled to climb the iron ladder that led towards a loft, which looked like a dungeon or a black hole. Tears were collecting in his eyes but he willed his emotions into a stoic frozen state and when he couldn't take it anymore left the place fighting hard to maintain his composure and sanity

Tiwari stood outside Shabnam hotel smoking a cigarette. The moment he saw Asif approaching, he threw his half burnt cigarette but before he could ask any questions Asif walked past him and sat on the last table.

"Tiwari, I have found Jenny, she is there and we need to get her out."

It brought a smile on Tiwari's face but seeing a somber Asif he quickly withdrew his smile. Asif looked at him with ire and said, "Let's not go to the police as you had rightly said, it would be of no use and besides Jenny's father also does not want it either."

"Then, what do we do? We will have to lead an invasion of at least thousand men to get her out of this wretched place" argued Tiwari. A tenacious Asif remained silent as all kinds of thoughts crossed his mind, he wasn't sure what he was going to do next.

He had promised Jenny that he would return the next day. That night he could not sleep. The moment he closed his eyes he would be faced with gory recurring images of her hollow eyes. He felt there were huge drums beating inside his head. He tried hard to sleep but kept twisting and turning and those horrible recurring images continued flashing in his mind making his head spin, sometimes he would think of ways of murdering Sudhakar but again his mind would fly back to Jenny's dreary waxen visage and thinking about how a tender girl who never ventured out of her small town was now waking up every day with drug addicts, alcoholics and the filthy dregs of Bombay city.

He dozed off for a while but woke up screaming when images of Jenny and her guttural voice resonated in his dream. He opened his eyes and was perspiring all over his body. He looked at the watch, it was four a.m. in the morning. He desperately wished to go to Pavalla street brothel and escape with Jenny. His mind was on a rollercoaster. Each minute brought a new thought. He was perspiring heavily and could feel palpitations, angina in his chest and pain of Jenny hammering in his head. The agony was unbearable and uncontrollable and he found it hard to lie in his bed any longer.

He looked at the watch. It was five a.m. he walked out of the house. Cool morning breeze hit his face. There were no vehicles on the road. The air was fresh as he sauntered towards the railway over bridge. The local trains had already started to ply and saw ChurchGate slow local train rumble onto the railway platform. There were very few passengers on the platform, some porters and laborers stood with their huge baskets.

He kept brooding about Jenny's fate especially with her fever and wondered how she would have spent the night in that horrible dark dungeon. He could not wait for daybreak and wanted to go to Jenny immediately. He was not sure if would able to assist her or to get her out but he could no longer bear the thought of her being in the state in which he had left her.

He stood watching the local trains for a long time and there was very little he could do to change things but painfully wait for the sun to rise. It was the longest morning of his life. The sun was shining much brighter. He returned home at seven thirty in the morning and then went straight to Tiwari's home and knocked the door. It took him ten minutes of banging the door to find half asleep Tiwari opening it with mucus in his eyes. Tiwari kept rubbing his eyes and peering at him in a semi-conscious state.

"Tiwari, go wash your face, we need to leave for Pavalla Street."

Tiwari groggily looked at his wrist watch and said, "Its early morning. They would also be sleeping"

"I don't know; we have to go there now. I need to check on Jenny." Tiwari rubbed his eyes and muttered, "Ok I will return in few minutes," saying he left inside.

Asif sat in his courtyard on charpoy a bed made of ropes. The moment he sat upon it, it sunk in like a hammock. The walls of the house were full of colorful pictures of Hindu Gods and Goddesses. The largest picture was of lord Shiva. He looked at the picture and thought Shiva looked magnificent. It was such an interesting picture. A blue complexioned broad shouldered Shiva sat on a Tiger's skin. Three lines on his forehead with a third eye in his temple. Long hair neatly rolled back and water spring symbolizing river Ganga emerging from it. A cobra snake coiled around his neck, a musical drum called 'Damru' in one of the many hands.

He was distracted when Pooja, Tiwari's younger sister walked in with tea in steel glass. He sipped tea and browsed at the rest of the pictures of gods on the wall. There was a picture of the Hindu God Hanuman, Goddess Durga sitting on a Tiger and last was the picture of Ganesha the elephant headed God. He continued to sip tea and observe the posters, meanwhile Tiwari walked in and looked a bit better yet his hair remained disheveled.

They took a taxi and headed straight to A-one brothel, Pavalla Street. It was early morning they walked briskly and swiftly and entered the decrepit building furtively. There were not too many people on the passage of the second floor and the main door was ajar. They entered the front hall and found a number of girls sleeping on the floor, some in their nightgowns and others merely wore just a long T-shirt. The room was full of women all over the floor. They watched them from outside the main door, most girls were fast asleep. A couple of them registered their presence but continued to sleep and did not bother to wake up.

Asif and Tiwari surveyed all the girls in the room but Jenny was not among them Tiwari slowly made his way towards the inner room, traipsing and very carefully balancing himself like walking over a minefield trying not to step over any of the sleeping women on the floor and Asif meticulously following his path.

He reached midway towards the door towards the other room when he accidently ended up kicking one of the sleeping women. She opened her eyes and furiously abused, "*Bhenchod* let me sleep." Tiwari was not amused. Walking precariously this time he continued to move forward towards the other room and Asif continued to follow his path. They reached the next room and realized there was some space to sleep in the other rooms yet most girls preferred to sleep in the main room. Perhaps it was an unwritten rule to use the inner rooms only for sex and not for sleeping.

Surprisingly there weren't any men present in the brothel at that time and most of the male pimps were missing. The temporary ladder leading to the top dark dungeon room that Jenny had used to climb to the top on previous night was missing. Asif wished to check the attic on top but it was not possible and attempting to go any further was risky business.

10

Tiwari looked for Sapna in the rooms but she was nowhere in sight, they returned to the main hall and looked at all the sleeping women. They were all sleeping on the floor like cattle in awkward poses. Some covered their face with *duppata* (veil) others slept with their hands on their faces. Both stood near the door and browsed the entire room, finally Tiwari was able to locate Sapna on the furthest corner of the room. He carefully made his way towards her and woke her up. She rubbed her eyes deliriously and was astonished to see Tiwari early morning. Unlike the other coquettish women of brothel, Sapna merely gave a cursory smile to Asif and her eyes and attention remained persistently focused on Tiwari. She quickly got up and both of them went behind one of the wooden partition sex rooms. Sapna continued to rub her eyes and sleepily spoke to Tiwari mischievously, "Did you get an erection early morning?"

"Look, Sapna I need your help," Tiwari replied and took her in the furthest corner, they spoke briefly and Sapna went back to sleep in the main hall. Tiwari did not divulge into too many details and gestured Asif to leave the place. Asif became increasingly impatient and once out of the main door he shot at Tiwari. "What happened? Tell me, what did you find out?" Tiwari lowered his head twitched his eye brows and said solemnly, "Well Asif, Jenny had a very high fever last night and they had to take her to Nair hospital."

Before Tiwari could say anything further he saw Asif scurried down tripping a few times over the wooden stair cases. Nair Hospital was not too far from Pavalla Street, they took a taxi and reached Nair Hospital in just a few minutes. There was the usual chaotic hustle and bustle native to any hospital with a large number of people streaming in and out, some ambulance blowing horn and patients being driven around on wheelchairs or ward boys moving patients on stretchers in and out.

They made their way towards the old building that had a stream of people standing in various queues in the Outdoor Patients Department or OPD waiting to register for their treatment. It was a Government charitable hospital and most of the patients belonged to the lowest strata of society.

There was no inquiry counter or any information desk available to assist anyone. The security guard sat in faded blue uniform near the entrance of stair case leading towards the patient's wards that were situated on higher floors of the building. The security guard sat on the wooden stool preparing his mixture of tobacco with a lot of dexterity. Then he stuffed a finger to place the tobacco on left side of his mouth that jutted by a slight lump. Asif moved forward and asked the guard the location of the ladies ward. The security guard answered, "*Chawbees* number." (Number twenty-four) No sooner did they begin to climb the steps of the old imperial building he stopped them. "You can't just go up like this at any hour, come back at visiting hours in the evening."

Asif removed a five rupee note from his front shirt pocket and placed it on security guard palms. The venal security guard pushed the note in his pocket and replied, "Fourth floor." Asif raced up the steps as his heart quickened. The odor of medicines pervaded the air and got more profound as they climbed higher on the massive steps. It was a huge edifice with numerous wards on each floor and there were no proper sign boards to indicate the female ward. A couple of ward boys stood talking to each other on the fourth floor. Asif asked them about ward for female patients. One of the ward boys pointed to the third ward on the left to the steps.

Asif stood outside and peeped inside the ward and noticed that there were numerous beds inside and most beds were in open but some were covered with green portable partition made of cloth. There were only women inside the ward and it was tough to enter the ladies ward in presence of the nurses or sisters. They stood outside the ward mulling ways of entering the ward when an old Ayah (Female ward assistant) walked up to them.

"What are you two doing here?"

"*Maoshi,* my wife is inside I want to see her."

"This is ladies ward; you must come in the visiting hours," snapped the woman in Marathi accented Hind. She glared at them with her wide eyes.

Asif realized she appeared an obtrusive woman and he implored, "*Maoshi,* my wife is alone, she needs me. I just arrived from my village. I have not even seen her. She needs me."

The Ayah's, tone softened as she spoke, "Ok, tell me her name?"

"Her name is Tara."

The *Ayah* did not say much but stormed into the ward. Asif waited patiently outside the ward and Tiwari got busy ogling at the passing Malayalee nurses.

The *Ayah* returned after ten minutes and said, "Ok, she is on bed number eight just keep in mind that the red belt senior nurse is not around so make sure you don't stay inside the ward in her presence."

Most nurses wore blue and the red belts to denote the sign of seniority. The red belts were dreaded by not only the patients and their relatives but also the junior nurses. They carried an arrogant stern aura and threw their weight around.

Asif thanked the Ayah and entered the ward furtively. Tiwari remained outside leering at the nurses. It was the Ladies general ward and most women belonged to poor households. Some were laborers and some others were prostitutes. The walls of the ward were full of dirty stains that had not been painted for years. The bed sheets were dirty and soiled. His heart was pounding fast as he made his way in. The ward was full of female patients. Some had oxygen masks on them others sat breast feeding their new born babies and upon seeing the male intrusion quickly covered their bosoms.

There wasn't much privacy for the patients. The beds were made of iron. The ceiling was very high and though there were fans of extra-long handles yet the air from the fans barely reached the beds. The fans made lot of grating noise and it was a miracle that they worked at all. He walked towards bed number eight. Jenny was sleeping all alone on the bed. Nobody from the brothel stayed by her side, they had simply dumped her in the hospital. Jenny was sleeping with a bottle of saline hanging by her bedside. She looked extremely weak and pallid. There was hardly any flesh on her body and she appeared like the remains of a badly damaged carcass. Asif touched her forehead and realized that she was burning with fever. His touch did not have any effect upon her; she appeared in a state of delirium.

Jenny lay on the bed with her eyes closed and was breathing noisily through her mouth in a semi-conscious state. There were some bandages on her hand that were indicative of the injections of various tests that were carried out upon her. Asif stood next to the bed and placed his hands on her forehead gently stroked her head. His heart sank as he watched her lay on the bed like a destitute. He wished he could croon her, place her head upon his lap and cradle her like a child and hold her in his arms.

A blue belt young nurse walked up to Jenny and started to check her blood pressure. "Sister what's the matter with her?" he asked her in English. That immediately drew her attention and she responded in heavily Malayalam accented English, "Her blood sample has been sent to the laboratory and the result should be out in sometime." The nurse spoke sympathetically as she had watched Asif caressing Jenny's forehead. The nurse appeared pale and her countenance reflected that she had an ominous feeling about Jenny's condition. Before leaving she warned him to leave the ward soon as it was ladies ward and he was not allowed to be there before the visiting hours.

Asif's hand was still on Jenny's forehead. He responded by thanking the nurse and assured her he would leave soon. The nurse left the bed and attended to the patient on the next bed. He could feel Jenny's burning body as fever encompassed her whole body. He wasn't sure if she was asleep or unconscious. He continued caressing her head while praying for her recovery. He was saying a silent prayer with his eyes closed when the silence was shattered by the shrill voice of a red belt senior nurse facing him.

"What are you doing here? This is ladies ward"

The entire ward was rattled by the fractious old woman's coarse harsh voice. Asif got up and in all politeness addressed the red belt nurse, "Sister, she is alone and has no one to look after her. Could you please let me stay for some time," he pleaded with his eyes begging for mercy but it had no effect upon the senior nurse who again launched a scathing verbal attack.

"Did you think this is a *Dharamshala?* (orphanage) You are not allowed to stay here for a minute. Just leave."

Everyone in the ward was startled and stared at him including the blue belt nurses. A helpless Asif had no choice but to leave. Arguing any further was pointless and could only make matters worse. He lowered his head and just as he started to withdraw his hands from Jenny's face, he felt Jenny holding his hand with her feeble fingers. He looked at her. She had faintly opened her eyes and murmured something. The entire ward witnessed in silence as Asif moved his ears closer to her face. Jenny whispered, "I Love you."

Tears rolled from his eyes he replied, "I love you too Jenny," and kissed her forehead, "Take Care. I will be back soon," so saying he pulled the bed sheet to swaddle her body till her neck. stoically covering his pain, he wiped his tears and slowly walked out of the ward.

Tiwari was still busy ogling the nurses and Ayahs when he noticed Asif and became attentive, "Is she okay? Asif merely shook his head and made his way towards the ground floor. They walked outside the hospital building. There were numerous people on the compound, doctors, interns, policemen and patients lying on stretchers. Asif kept walking numbly till they reached outside the hospital gates. They reached the main road and found that were no taxis on the road, he kept walking and saw a huge crowd standing at the bus stop waiting for BEST Buses.

Soon a double-decker bus rumbled towards the bus stop. Just as the bus was about to stop people broke all the norms and tried to hop inside the bus, Tiwari took lead and scampered inside the bus followed by Asif. There was total chaos some passengers who tried to get out of the bus were pushed back inside by those wanting to get inside; few managed to wriggle outside while the others abused. The bus stopped for less than a minute before they heard the double bell of the bus conductor.

The bus started to move. Tiwari had already entered the bus and Asif chased it for a while before he jumped and managed to hang on to the door handles. He balanced himself with one leg on the bus and other dangling in air. The bus reached near Mahalaxmi station. Asif jumped out much before the bus could stop to avoid incoming rush. The bus came to in grinding halt, the passengers rushed in and Tiwari managed to squeeze out of the melee. Once out of the bus instead of walking towards home Asif began to walk on the other side.

"Where are you going?" asked Tiwari.

"I don't know. I just want to be left alone".

Tiwari scratched his stubble and said, "Don't be alone. I will be with you," and began walking along with him "Where do you want to go?"

"I don't know I just want to be away till five pm because that's the time I can visit Jenny."

Tiwari pretended to chew some imaginary tobacco in his mouth and said, "Alright, let's go to Mahalaxmi Temple." They walked all the way in spite of the bright shining sun and they made their way towards the Mahalaxmi Temple. It took them 15 minutes to reach the Temple. Some Gujarati businessmen were throwing grains to the pigeons that were feeding on the ground outside the compound. Numerous Sadhus in their saffron robes walked in and out of the Temple premises. On the way towards the main Temple complex they came across some smaller Temples leading towards the waterfront.

Crestfallen Asif kept walking in his stupor and did not notice Tiwari sneaking into a smaller temple and return with some crushed *Bhang* (cannabis) leaves that he bought from one of the Sadhus. They found a place to sit under the shade near the main temple complex, myriads of pilgrims kept entering and exiting the Temple. Tiwari got some sweets from a nearby shop and quickly opened the *Bhang* packet and offered some of it to Asif who refused. Tiwari did not push him any further and quickly swallowed the ball of succulent *Bhang* with water.

Asif spoke very little and kept to himself watching the people walk by. Tiwari went on a sweet gorging spree starting with *Peda, Jalebi* and topped it with a glass of tea. After an hour Tiwari was completely intoxicated and high on effects of *Bhang*. Asif sat brooding under the shed while Tiwari was on a roll with his antics and quirks reeling under the effects of *Bhang*. He would walk around, return with a smile or laugh aimlessly and start walking again. He went inside the Temple infinite times and at last Asif lost count of the number of times Tiwari went for *Darshan*. Sometimes he would keep staring at a female devotee's bottom and stayed in that position long after the woman had left the place.

He repeatedly went inside the temple and after ringing the bell walked out, once again walked in ringing the bell. One of the Temple priests got irked by his antics and emerged out of the temple but in a change of heart decided to ignore him and go back inside the temple to collect the offerings.

Asif felt pain of angina in his chest and was getting breathless. He kept looking at the watch and wished evening would come sooner. Every girl in the temple premises reminded him of Jenny. Not the school girl of his memories that he believed for years had spurned his love but the waxen girl who was nothing more than a living carcass lying unattended in ladies' general ward of Nair hospital.

He checked the time it was three pm, still couple of hours before he could see Jenny. The sun was sliding downwards but the heat was still on. Some people made their way towards the rocky sea beach behind the Temple. Tiwari had already made a few rounds of the beach in the scorching heat. Asif made his way towards the water and Tiwari joined him. "C'mon let's go to the water," grinned Tiwari kicking a coconut on the ground. Asif in spite of being totally shattered with trauma was not offended by Tiwari's silly behavior. He knew his demeanor since childhood and was aware that Tiwari may have been high on *Bhang*, flirting with girls and monkeying around yet he was always there when he needed him and never abandoned him, even in the worst of situations.

They made their way towards the rocky beach. The sun descended towards horizon yet it was still warm and bright. A large number of people sat on the black rocks. The sea waves clashed with the rock, some women and children sat with their families. The young lover couples were deeper in the sea and sat strategically behind the bigger rocks and boulders. Tiwari was still very high on the effects of Bhang. He would walk up to Asif to strike a conversation but his visage would remind him of his trauma and he would leave him alone to get on with other interests like leering at women or being voyeuristic towards some couples.

Asif checked his watch. It was four thirty p.m., just thirty minutes to go. When it was time to leave he looked around for Tiwari who was nowhere to be seen. He went to check at the Temple he wasn't there either. He was getting increasingly impatient and he wanted to rush to hospital soon but Tiwari was missing. He wondered if Tiwari had gone back to the Sadhu to get some more dosage of Bhang. He went towards the smaller Temple where Tiwari had got the Bhang. Two bearded Sadhus sat smoking pot, the smell of weed was in the air but Tiwari remained missing.

A frustrated Asif decided to go back and check the beach once again. The sun was down and there were many more people on the beach that meant it was going to be difficult to locate Tiwari. After making several rounds of the temple complex, finally he spotted a shirtless Tiwari standing waist deep inside the sea waves. He stood watching him from over the rocks flabbergasted, he wondered if he should chide him or just leave him on his own on the shore and rush to hospital. Tiwari saw him and asked for his hand for support to get him out of water. Asif shrugged his head and pulled him out of water, "What do you think you were doing inside water? Do you know to swim?" Tiwari nodded in negative. He did not ask him any further questions and dragged him out.

They reached the main road and caught a taxi. Tiwari completely drenched in sea water sat on the back seat. It was the evening rush hour and traffic moved at snail's pace. Normally it would take not more than twenty minutes to reach but on that day it had taken almost an hour to reach the hospital. It was almost forty-five minutes past five. He paid the taxi fare and almost ran towards Jenny's ward. The place was full of patients and their relatives walking in and out, he ran towards the third floor bumping and brushing against others. He rushed straight into the ladies ward towards Jenny's bed but she was missing. He looked around desperately but could not find her. He searched for any on duty nurse or doctor to inquire about her but there were none.

He kept looking for her from bed to bed with no avail. Distraught he looked for her helplessly all over the ward but could not trace her. Suddenly the female patient on the next bed spoke, "She has been shifted to intensive care unit. The moment he heard that he made a mad dash out of the ward but the moment he stepped out he realized he did not know the location of intensive care unit. He saw the same Ayah who he had bumped into in the morning walking in and he asked her, "*Maoshi* where is the Intensive care unit?" The *Ayah* told him that intensive care unit or ICU was in the new building.

He knew that new building was at quite a distance, situated behind the parking space and medical college building. He needed to cover a lot of ground to reach there. He rushed towards the new building. Tiwari stood on the steps, watched him dash and quickly followed him. Some people stopped to watch them. Asif ran forward followed by Tiwari chasing him all over the hospital. The chase ended when they reached the new building. Tiwari could not match up to his pace but still managed to reach the location. Asif stood panting outside the intensive care unit situated on the ground floor.

A security guard in blue uniform sat on a wooden stool outside the ICU. It was an enclosed room with a huge heavy metallic door. The security guard watched a breathless Asif and realizing the urgency asked, "Who is the patient?"

"My wife Tara is very serious and I need to see her," he gasped between short breaths.

The security guard was sympathetic yet firm. He answered in a conciliatory manner "You cannot spend a lot of time inside? It's the intensive care unit."

"I know, I just need to see her and speak to the doctor about her condition," Asif pleaded.

The security guard opened the huge door, Asif entered the intensive care unit. It was much cleaner than the general ward. He walked up straight towards the on duty nurse who was writing some patient's case history.

Asif spoke in English, "Sister, my wife goes by the name of Tara. She has been admitted here, can you please tell me about her? The nurse raised her head and said "She has been diagnosed with a severe case of pneumonia and is in a very critical condition. You can see her but please do not try to speak to her." The nurse reflected immense compassion in her voice which was so rare in government hospitals where myriads of nameless patients are brought in everyday; some survive while others are namelessly taken out to meet their creator.

"Can I see her?" he begged

"Yes, you can. But don't speak to her or spend much time here," saying she pointed towards the right hand corner and continued to write again

A frail and pallid Jenny lay on bed with all sorts of medical equipment's beeping around her. She looked worse than she did in the morning. An oxygen mask covered her mouth and there was unusual movement of her stomach as she breathed in and out.

When Asif emerged out of the ICU he saw Tiwari standing outside. Tiwari looked into his eyes and asked, "What happened?" A forlorn Asif replied that Jenny has been diagnosed with a severe case Pneumonia and she was in a very serious condition. Tiwari was still under the influence of Bhang yet maintained a great degree of sobriety.

Asif couldn't do much apart from waiting and praying for her recovery. He slumped in one of the corners of the passage outside the ICU. A few other patients' relatives sat on the platforms made of granite stones and looked at him with conceit as he was the only one sitting on the floor with his back to the wall. The floor was dirty and the walls full of stains of paan and tobacco but at the moment he was beyond any compulsion of etiquettes or prissiness.

He sat in that squalid corner for next three hours motionless. Tiwari in the meantime had checked most of the building still reeling under effects of Bhang. Around nine p.m. a visibly exhausted Tiwari slumped next to him and urged him to join him for dinner at the local canteen. Asif refused to move and instead asked Tiwari to go home and return the next morning.

A stoned Tiwari sat on the floor staring at the old ceiling fan and flapping his hands in the air like wings, the Bhang was yet having its effect upon him. "Tiwari please go home and sleep, you are still high on Bhang," Asif requested him. Tiwari stopped moving his hands in the air and spoke, "Yes I ate a lot of sweets and I should not have drunk the tea. That just made it worse, but I am fine. Let me stay here." Asif insisted that he went home. He got up stared at Asif for a long time and walked out of the building.

Asif was oblivious to happenings around him. He sat motionless in the dirty corner of the room crossed legged with his head placed on this knees. Relatives and kin of patients continued coming and going out of the hospital. Most of them had gloomy visage. There was nothing to smile about outside the ICU. There would be an occasional rare happy face when someone received the news of recovery of their loved ones, rest was rather caliginous.

It was one a.m. and only a few people remained in the hall way, A Bihari woman of dusky complexion sat on the stone bench with her little boy that was not more than four or five years old. She was rather nervous being the only woman around. Two other men of the *Wagri* community of Gujarat Saurashtra kept moving in and out of the hall. They were inebriated and reeling under the influence of alcohol which could be felt from a distance yet they intended no malice towards anyone.

At around one thirty a.m. the *Wagri* men decided to lie down on the ground. They spread a bed sheet on the floor and went to sleep. An apparently drunk short ward boy with a whitish complexion stumbled down from staircase and stood tremulously in his white uniform. He scanned the entire room. The *Wagri* men were fast asleep. He leered at the Bihari woman for a long time making her uncomfortable.

The ward boy glanced at Asif and walked up to him and asked, "Do you want anything? I can get food for you," Asif nodded his head in negative, the ward boy spoke again, "I can get you beer, just give me the money and it will be done." Asif was getting vexed by this man and told him to leave. The ward boy stood for some time and then blasted "What do these guys think this is some kind of charity?" so saying he angrily stomped out of the room. Had it been any other situation, Asif would have gone hard at the man for the insult but at the moment he did not have the will nor the stomach to indulge into any act of retribution.

Mosquitoes and flies buzzed all over the room, they kept biting him yet he could not do much about it. He found himself helpless and unable to palliate Jenny in any way and all he could do was just pray to God for Jenny's health.

It was three in the morning and there was pin drop silence in the room, except for the snores of one of the Wargi men. The Bihari woman was in a drowsy state when suddenly the door of ICU opened and the ward boy walked out and walked up to Asif and said, "Are you with Tara?"

Asif got up rubbing his eyes and answered, "Yes I am".

The ward boy wiped his forehead with handkerchief and spoke in a somber tone, "She is dead." You can inform your family and collect her body in the morning. He must have performed this dreadful act of breaking this most unfortunate news about deceased patients through the years over and over again and it had become a routine job ritual for him yet it was a difficult moment for him and he could not stand facing Asif for long, hence he turned and walked back into the ICU slamming the door.

Asif stood facing the metallic ICU door for a long time. There were no tears in his eyes. He felt his legs would crack into a thousand pieces and he would not be able to move. He thought his heart was going to explode and his head felt heavy and spun leaving him completely blinded and in a flash he fainted on the ground.

The Bihari woman and two *Wagri* men who had by then woken up rushed towards him. One of the men splashed water on his face. Asif opened his eyes and saw blurred faces of one of the men holding him and he slowly balanced himself on his feet. The woman kept saying, "It's all a matter of destiny and the will of God." If he was a weaker man he would have beat his chest and wailed till he tore his hair out but he did not respond to any of their condolences and slowly walked out of the room and the hospital.

None of the brothel inmates or acquaintances bothered to check on Jenny. She was shifted to the mortuary. She had to be laid to rest for her final valediction and her interment. Asif went to the nearest STD booth, phoned one of his cousins in Mangalore and dictated him the telephone number of Babu Bhai's hotel. He requested him to pass the number to Mr. Rodriguez and ask him to call urgently on that number. Asif waited the entire day for Mr. Rodriguez's call at the hotel. The phone rang at four p.m., Mr. Rodriguez was on the phone. Asif conveyed the sad news to him and asked him to come to Bombay immediately for Jenny's funeral service.

There was a long silence on the other end Mr. Rodriguez responded in a cracked voice that he would reach as soon as possible.

Mr. Rodriguez arrived directly at the mortuary of Nair Hospital a day after being informed as it took twenty-four hours for the journey from Mangalore to Bombay by bus. Asif was already waiting for him. He did not look into Asif's eyes nor did he ask any questions about the circumstances or events leading to her death. He kept prevaricating and looked at ground as he spoke, "I will make preparations for the funeral." He left the hospital soon after.

He returned a few hours later with a hearse van owned by Pinto undertakers. Asif meanwhile took care of the paperwork and handed out generous bribes for the small mercies of the hospital staff. It was six p.m. A couple of hospital ward boys were paid ten rupees each for carrying Jenny's body to the black hearse.

The body was brought out and placed inside the hearse. It was the first time Mr. Rodriguez saw Jenny's face ever since she had left the house. The ward boys shoved the body from the stretcher rather recklessly into the wooden casket lying in the hearse van. Jenny's face was briefly visible before the casket was shut. Tiwari sat next to the driver. Mr. Rodriguez and Asif sat across each other at the back of the van with casket in between them.

The hearse rumbled its way outside the hospital. Mr. Rodriguez had his face buried in his palms while Asif kept staring at the casket. It was the evening rush hour and the hearse van would often stop with a jerk and the casket would shake. Asif wondered if Jenny felt discomfort inside the coffin. It was foolish, he knew she was dead and she could no longer feel any pain, all her emotions, feelings and physical torments had ceased to exist. She was just a lifeless cadaverous corpse inside the wooden casket.

The hearse reached the Haines road Catholic cemetery. Mr. Rodriguez got down of the van and he joined him. The undertaker who was waiting for them joined them along with an unknown man as they carried the wooden coffin inside the picturesque cemetery. The cemetery was covered with greenery and numerous graves with gravestones on them. The coffin was carried to a small church built inside the burial ground for the funeral service. A priest in spotless white robe stood inside the church.

Mr. Rodriguez, the chapel and the undertaker went inside the cemetery church for the requiem service before the burial. Asif stayed outside the church. Mr. Rodriguez turned and looked at him with crinkled eyes, a kind of gesture that expected him to join the service but he chose to stay outside.

After sometime they emerged out of the church. Asif rushed forward to assist them in carrying the coffin towards the fresh grave that had been already dug by the mortician in the furthest corner of the cemetery. The casket was laid beside the grave before being lowered down in the final resting place. The undertaker opened the casket for the last time. Jenny's face was cold yet beautiful, her sea blue beautiful angelic eyes were shut forever. It was the moment Mr. Rodriguez broke down and began to wail. The priest read the prayers haltingly with a religious book in his left hand and comforted him with the right hand.

Asif was overwhelmed with emotions. He felt piercing pain in his chest and darkness before his eyes and felt he was about to pass out. It was hard for him to control himself and felt he would collapse on the ground. He crumbled on his knees slumping on the muddy ground and balanced himself to sit in a crossed legged position. The undertaker entered the grave a few feet below the ground. The body was interred. The priest continued to chant the prayers and within no time undertaker started to fill the grave with mud. Within few minutes everything was over. The priest walked away towards the church. The two other men walked towards the tap to wash themselves. Persistent streams of tears continued to flow from Mr. Rodriguez's eyes as he sat near the grave with his head lowered. Asif touched the ground and it sank into him that Jenny was no more. All her dreams and afflictions were over and she was a lifeless corpse buried under six feet under the ground. Mr. Rodriguez sat weeping next to the grave but it was unbearable for Asif. His soul cried for oblivion and could no longer bear the trauma. He kissed Jenny's grave and dragged himself out of the cemetery.

11

Sudhakar Shetty was an owner of many dance bars in Bombay. One of the most well-known amongst them was Diamond Crown besides few others in the suburbs called Moonlight dance and Moonshine. These dance bars were supposed to be meant for entertainment but it was a well-known fact that apart from that it was also notorious for prostitution. He had employed many Mangalorean boys in his hotels some of them were his relative's and others were from poorer families from his native village of Kinnikoli.

He was a resident of a plush apartment in Andheri, where he had shifted some years ago from Sion a place where he had spent the early part of his years in Bombay. Sudhakar had made many enemies, destroyed many lives in his surge for building his evil empire and was not an easy man to take on.

In Mangalore, he was known as a simple decent family man, but in reality he was a very powerful man with many muscle men working for him and with powerful connections. The local ministers and corporators belonging to different political parties paid obeisance to him.

His patrons included the local police inspector and many other top police officials. Sudhakar made a huge fortune in dance bars. He greased the palms of the police willingly and one of his close friends was a top trigger happy cop who was an infamous but decorated encounter specialist.

Asif was a street smart young man living in Bombay city. He knew a few boys from the notorious Pathari chawl in Saath Rasta and also a few foot soldiers connected to the company in Bhendi Bazaar, yet he was in no position to take on the might of powerful Sudhakar Shetty.

Sudhakar was capable of destroying him without leaving any trace and Asif was fully aware of that, forbearance became his mantra as he realized he would have to think hard before taking any step against the powerful man.

The next few days were absolute nightmare but he had to move forward. Asif began planning ways of attaining his retribution and making Sudhakar Shetty pay for destroying his Jenny's life. He had an overwhelming desire for revenge. At times he would wake up in middle of his sleep and with strong impulsion to just murder him. He thought of multiple ways of murdering Sudhakar and facing the consequences but better sense would prevail and he would swallow his pain. Sometimes thoughts of stabbing Sudhakar whenever and wherever he got a chance would cross his mind but again felt it would be suicidal if he failed and botched up his mission to kill Sudhakar or in case he got arrested by police his temerity could prove costly.

He began collecting every bit of information about Sudhakar. He learned that one of his daughters studied in Lala Lajpatrai College and the younger one studied at Harkishan School in Andheri. He also briefly thought of kidnapping one of his daughters but his compassionate heart dismissed that vicious plan. But he found it harder and harder with each passing day to bear the resonating waves of anger that kept hitting him repeatedly. He wanted Sudhakar to suffer and pay for his evil deeds and that was the only mission and purpose in his life. He was not able to sleep in nights with fury at the same time he was aware that he was helpless and could not afford to act impetuously

Memories of Jenny haunted him and it was getting increasingly painful for him. He could not breathe freely and bear the agony. He tried to find more information about Sudhakar and spent time gathering every detail he could find. One day Asif retrieved an important piece of information from a man called Babu Bhai an old Malbari cook who worked at Abdul Khader's restaurant at Temkar Street.

Babu Bhai had known Sudhakar since his boyhood days when Sudhakar had arrived to Bombay from Mangalore. Babu Bhai and Sudhakar had worked together in the hotel years ago. While Sudhakar had risen to become a successful entrepreneur, poor Babu Bhai remained a mere cook throughout his life and was miles behind his devious erstwhile colleague.

Babu Bhai worked in the kitchen everyday till one thirty a.m. and slept only for three hours before he would wake up again at five a.m. to serve tea to the customers in the morning. He would drink country liquor every night and that was the only time for his recreation.

Asif reached Abdul's hotel at one a.m. He carried a bottle of whiskey and some delectable fried fish that he had bought outside Dadar railway station. He waited for the hotel to shut down and finally at two a.m., the shutters came down. He made his way towards the door from back of the kitchen. Babu Bhai sat smoking beedi on a jute gunny sack in a corner.

"How are you, Babu Bhai?" he asked amiably as he sat next to him and removed the bottle of whisky. Babu Bhai was a dark man with a hoarse voice and a pot belly that made him look very ugly. He was so exhausted with the day's work that he did not bother to ask any questions or seek answers about the unexpected feast that he was being treated with and he straight away reached for the bottle and poured it into the steel glass that he removed from his bag.

Babu Bhai gulped in the first peg in a flash and began to devour the fried fish. Asif poured some whisky into his emptied glass. He asked him questions about his younger days and his early life in Bombay. Babu Bhai ate and drank greedily as if it was the last drop and morsel on the planet. After drinking the second glass he felt relaxed, pushed his back against the wall with his shirt dripping with perspiration and looked towards Asif with some interest and started talking "I came to Bombay the day Mahatma Gandhi was killed. I was a small boy. I don't remember much except sitting on the back of a truck from Kerala." In a short while he started sharing his stories with a flurry of garbled words.

Asif wasn't interested in listening to any of his biography or anecdotes yet he feigned listening intently. Meanwhile Babu Bhai had finished the entire bottle in no time. Pushing the empty bottle in a corner he got up and removed a plastic pouch from his bag and said, "Hey this is *phooga* (country liquor) It's much better than your English stuff," and started to pour the liquor into the glass. "Anna is it true that you once worked for Sudhakar?" Babu Bhai paused looked up and spat on the ground in contempt "Thoo, I, worked for that bastard? No. That Bhadwa used to work with me when I worked for Mallesh Kamati. Both of us worked for Mallesh Kamati," Asif pushed some peanuts towards him and asked, "Who's Mallesh Kamati?"

Babu Bhai poured whisky in the steel glass, "Mallesh Anna was a very simple and kind man. He owned a restaurant near Rani Baugh Byculla. I was his main cook and that cockroach

Sudhakar was a young boy. He was a sweeper and sometimes worked as a waiter. Mallesh Anna was a very kind soul. He paid us on time and always looked after our welfare. He even supported that serpent Sudhakar to get his education. He got him admission in night school and also paid his fees and look, how the viper, bit him!" He gulped the contents of the entire glass.

"Babu Bhai, tell me more about Mallesh Kamati"

Babu Bhai removed a packet of 30 number brand beedi from his shirt pocket and after lighting one beedi exhaled the smoke across Asif's face. The strong beedi smoke made him uneasy and he could not breathe easily yet he did not want to change his position or leave the place and distract Babu Bhai's flow of words.

"Mallesh Anna occasionally smoked Ganja and he would send Sudhakar to get his regular dose of Ganja. The conniving bastard got Mallesh Anna hooked to it. Sudhakar would get more packets than required from Dharavi slums for Mallesh Anna till there came a time that he got so addicted that he never came out of it. Soon he got hooked on to it and began smoking it every day. He was so highly addicted that he spent more time smoking than sitting in the hotel. Sudhakar cunningly took his place to sit on the counter instead as Mallesh Anna would be stoned most of the time. To make matters worse as a result of excessive drugs he also became impotent. The treacherous serpent seduced his wife and in no time not only took over his wife but also his restaurant."

Babu Bhai paused to poured some more liquor in the glass and quaffed it,

"So does that mean Sudhakar lives with Mallesh Anna's wife?" asked Asif.

"Huh!" Smirked Babu with glowering eyes and said, "She disappeared many years ago along with her son. No one has heard about them. The bastard got a new younger wife from his native Mangalore."

"What about Mallesh Anna?" Asif persisted

"Mallesh Anna!" he sighed dolefully, "No one knows about him. He is a destitute, a vagabond. He picks rags and smokes drugs rest of the time with whatever money that he makes by selling rags." Asif paused for a moment.

"Where can I find him?" inquired Asif cautiously.

"Young man, there is no permanent haven for such a homeless destitute *charsi*." (drug addict)

"When did you see him for the last time?" asked Asif.

Babu Bhai's puckered his face full of wrinkles, scratched his beard and looked at Asif's face for a long time and said, "I saw him last year at Bombay Central station with some drug addicts." Four glasses had already been emptied. He peered at his empty glass and said, "Do you have some more whisky?" Asif got up placed a hundred rupees note in his shirt pocket and walked out of the restaurant.

Next morning, Asif reached Bombay Central station along with Tiwari. He had often observed some *Gardullah's* (Heroin addicts) sitting near platform number one below the bridge. He asked Tiwari to wait on platform number two, as he jumped and crossed the railway tracks towards platform number one under the bridge. He entered the alley between platform number one and across a playground, it was a dirty passageway used by drug addicts and recidivists reeking with feces and litter.

Two gaunt rag picker boys who were not more than fifteen years of age sat smoking brown sugar in a corner. One of them held a silver foil in his hand while the other burnt the lighter.

As they noticed Asif approach near them they hesitated a bit and tried to hide the silver foil behind their back.

Asif flashed his smile in a bid to pacify them and make them feel assured but they were suspicious of his motives and remained on the edge.

"Hi! I am Asif; do you guys by chance know Mallesh Kamati? Both the boys looked at each other. He asked again, "Do you know Mallesh Kamati? He's a *Gardulla* like you."

One of the boys with a hollow clavicle took umbrage to his use of word *Gardulla* for them and with a withering look shot back, "We don't know any Mallesh, Vallesh get lost."

Asif could see Tiwari sitting across on platform number two. He was incensed with the affronting remark of the kid and for a second thought of kicking the boy across his face but took a deep breath and swallowed the insult. Ignoring the recalcitrant *Gardullah* boys he looked around and noticed an old drug addict gawking at him through his drooping eyes from a distance. The man was covered with a blanket with his back to the wall. The weather was hot and humid yet the man was under the blanket.

He walked up to the old man, "Do you know Mallesh Kamati?" The old man raised his head out of blanket looking at him point blank and spoke in his gravelly voice,

"What would I get if, I tell you the answer?"

Asif saw a ray of hope in the old man and he quickly reached for the pocket and removed a fifty rupee note and offered it to the old man.

The old man looked at the fifty rupees note and scoffed "What do you think, I am, a *chindi chor*?" saying he looked the other way contemptuously.

Asif removed another hundred rupees note and offered it to him. The old man pushed the money under the sack made of jute that he was sitting upon and started to speak, "You can find *Mallya* at the Worli *kabristan*." (Cemetery) Go there at midnight and you will find him." Asif was aware that there were at least three or more cemeteries in Worli "Which kabristan, are you talking about?" The old man in his hoarse voice retorted, *"Arrey chutiya, woh Yahudi kabristan, worli wala."* The old man once again covered himself with the blanket and started smoking brown sugar.

Asif understood that he was mentioning the Jewish Cemetery that was located in Dr. E Moses Road Worli.

Asif left his home at half past ten in the night. Tiwari was already waiting for him under the building. He started the bike and they made their way towards Worli. Their first stop was Poonam Bar near Worli naka.

They made their way towards the Worli sea face but once again stopped at Himalaya heights building to buy a bottle of beer from the wine shop. Soon they reached Worli sea face and could see a number of people on the promenade. A few boys and couples sat on the rocks deeper inside the sea. Some people were jogging along the sea side. As usual the hawkers sold peanuts, *bhelpuri* to coconut water on the roadside.

They made themselves comfortable on the rocks. Tiwari opened the beer bottle with his mouth. They sat drinking beer by the moonlight and watched few eunuchs harassing couples for money at a distance. One of the Eunuchs tried to approach them but stop midway after seeing that they were not one of the lover couple.

Soon it was near midnight. Asif started the bike and raced towards Mahalaxmi station, they crossed the Worli naka, Racecourse wall was on the right and Jewish cemetery on left. Asif had used this road many a times but had never ever bothered to venture anywhere near the Jewish cemetery. He stopped his bike outside the cemetery gate. Parking it on the main stand he began to push open the cemetery gates.

Tiwari was horrified seeing Asif opening the gates of the graveyard and pleaded "What's wrong with you? Please do not go inside, I am scared." Asif looked at him and answered, "Tiwari, stay with me." Tiwari was petrified and began to snivel; Asif was already inside the burial ground. He held Tiwari's hand with one hand and continued walking in. It was a very old Jewish graveyard that was in use more than fifty years ago when there was a sizeable Jewish population in the city but now most Jews had left for Israel hence the graveyard only had old graves, hardly used in recent years.

Most of the graves were as old as hundred years, some of the graves were in bad shape, few had their gravestones missing yet amazingly most of the grave stones were in impeccable state. They kept walking in among the graves and when they reached the end of the burial ground. Suddenly from behind one of grave stones emerged a shady man in dirty clothes. As he came nearer Tiwari stopped whining and froze. The man drew near them, in the full moon night his face was very clear he had a dark face and beard covered most of his face. He looked towards Asif and Tiwari and asked "Did you guys bring any 'maal?' (Stuff)

Asif remained calm and asked, "You are Mallesh Anna?" The man was surprised to hear his name and asked,

"Who sent you here?"

Asif asked again, "Are you, Mallesh Anna?"

The man did not answer him. It appeared that he was about to turn around and leave but suddenly he lurched forward charging towards them with his hands attempting to strangle them. Asif made a swift left turn to dodge him and as a result the old man fell on his face. Asif grabbed his hands pulled them on his back. The man put up a struggle, screamed and tried to free him so that he could attack again. Asif struggled with him and pinned him on the ground. A startled Tiwari stood watching in shock from a distance. Asif shot loudly, "Tiwari hold him!"

A reluctant Tiwari came forward to assist him and pinned Mallesh Anna's head on ground. Mallesh Anna gave out a horrible scream. Tiwari in a panic withdrew and stood shakily in corner leaving Asif grappling with the man. Mallesh Anna tried to rise but Asif held him by his arms around his back and blasted Tiwari, "Idiot, help me! Hold him."

Tiwari came forward and grasped to hold Mallesh Anna's arms. He was an old man and soon got exhausted grappling and gave it up. They had completely overpowered him and he lay panting on the ground.

Mallesh Anna kept hollering wildly and again tried to extract himself from their clutches in vain. Asif tried to calm him down by talking to him but he would not relent. The man was afraid, paranoid and had total mistrust towards their intentions.

"Mallesh Anna! Mallesh Anna! I intent no harm to you, don't be afraid, we are not here to harm you."

Mallesh Anna was an old man, he was tired and gave up struggling to escape and lay motionless on the ground. There was an impasse for a while which gave a breather to all. Asif helped Mallesh Anna sit on the ground and quickly pinned his hands behind his back like a prisoner.

Mallesh Anna sat on the ground with his head facing the ground, his long unkempt wild hair covering his face completely. It appeared that he had capitulated and given up. Tiwari stood facing him and said "Anna, relax! You don't have to worry; we are here to help you." He reached for his trouser pockets and removed a packet of cigarettes. After removing a solitary cigarette, he threw the empty packet away. He placed the cigarette on his lips and tried burning it with a match stick. He failed in his first attempt and tried to light it the second time.

Just as Tiwari was about to burn the cigarette, Mallesh Anna gave a loud growl and lunged forward and bit Tiwari on his thighs. Tiwari groaned and yelped as Mallesh Anna had dug his teeth deep into flesh. Asif tried to pull Mallesh Anna back but he would not let Tiwari go. He hit Mallesh Anna hard with his elbow and as result he fell on his back. Asif overpowered Mallesh Anna again and held him by his hands.

Tiwari was in pain, he kept howling and cried aloud with blood dripping all over his trousers and on the ground. It was a bright moonlit night and the blood could be seen all over the ground. Mallesh Anna kept snarling like a wolf and his clenched teeth dripped blood. Tiwari was in a rage and hissing in fury after being bitten, charged towards the old man and kicked Mallesh Anna across his face sending him crashing on the ground and hitting a gravestone.

Asif who was holding him also tumbled along but did not let go of Mallesh Anna hands. He quickly gathered himself and Mallesh Anna and yelled, "Tiwari, have you gone mad?" Tiwari was fuming with anger and returned to attack one more time. "Stop it, Tiwari. Are you, insane? The man is an old drug addict, a desolate, just leave him alone," pleading he shielded Mallesh Anna by covering him with his hands. Tiwari stopped his charge and stood breathing heavily yet still fuming with rage and groaning in pain with the grossly injured thigh.

Asif tried to mollify him, "Tiwari you need to get a bandage for your wound and also get a rope to tie this man." Tiwari stood panting, breathlessly and paused for a long time. He inspected his injury. It was very bad. He winced in pain, cogitated for a while, gulped the saliva in his mouth and whimpered, "Okay! I will return with a rope and lasso this wild beast." Dragging himself slowly he made his way out of the graveyard.

12

Mallesh Anna sat in a motionless repose with his head facing the ground and Asif firmly held his hands behind his back in complete silence. The only sound that could be heard was that of Mallesh Anna breathing heavily along with the crickets and other nocturnal insects in the cemetery. He could hear an occasional sound of a passing vehicle on the road or some barking mongrel within the cemetery. Asif was worried that if Mallesh Anna attempted to struggle once again he would find it difficult to subdue him alone and prayed that Mallesh Anna remained calm and wished that Tiwari would return soon with the rope.

Tiwari's blow had softened Mallesh Anna like a frazzled boxer who was knocked out and had no energy left for another bout.

Asif looked at his watch; it was thirty-five minutes past two in the morning. Nearly forty minutes had passed since Tiwari left. He was at some distance from the graveyard entrance gate but was still able to spot any vehicle that stopped outside the graveyard. He could see an occasional taxi or a truck pass on the main road. It was getting increasingly cold. The ground was wet with the dew. His throat was dry and he felt completely parched and enervated.

He felt hopeful and gave a sigh of relief when he heard the sound of a taxi stop at some distance from the graveyard gate. A visibly drunk Tiwari entered the graveyard and this time around surprisingly did not reflect any fear that he displayed the first time he entered the graveyard. He walked straight towards them with a rope in his left hand and bottle of water on his right. Asif was glad that Tiwari got some water along. "Yaar, give me some water. My throat is running dry."

Tiwari winked. "It's not water. It's a Whisky Mix!"

Asif was surprised and said, "For God's sake Tiwari, we are in this graveyard at this hour and you think it's time to drink whisky?"

"This beast has chewed a lot of meat out of me. I need to alleviate the pain," muttered Tiwari. Asif grabbed the bottle drank, some whisky and instantly felt invigorated. He looked towards Mallesh Anna and asked him, "Anna, do you want water?"

There was no response. Mallesh Anna had been immobile with a head down position for a long time and his face was completely covered with his thick hair that had grown long because of years of not being cut.

They tied his hands behind the back that allowed Asif to use both his hands. He tried to speak to Mallesh Anna, "Anna do you want to drink water?"

Tiwari did not want to take another risk and stayed cautiously at safe distance. There was no response from Mallesh Anna. Asif placed the bottle in front of him and waited for Mallesh Anna to react but he did not move and lay in the same position motionless. He was in no position to assault or escape with his hands tied behind his back yet he was capable of biting again.

"Tiwari, we need to give him something to drink."

"Asif be careful. The animal can strike again," snapped Tiwari.

Asif moved forward and tremulously pushed Mallesh Anna's hair behind his back and tried to feed him some whisky. He was shocked to see Mallesh Anna bleeding profusely and his face covered with blood. Apparently, Tiwari's kick had caused great damage. He probably had a broken jaw and appeared to be in a bad state.

"Mallesh Anna! Mallesh Anna!"

Asif tried to get him to talk but Mallesh Anna remained speechless and appeared to have fainted.

Asif let his guard down and held Mallesh Anna's head with his one hand and tried to feed him whisky by placing the water bottle on his mouth. He responded by drinking slowly, which was a positive sign. It brought some relief to Asif, yet Mallesh Anna's condition was a cause of concern. He was hurt badly and needed some medical attention.

Tiwari continued maintaining a cautious distance and avoided proximity to Mallesh Anna,

"Tiwari, the man is badly injured. Come here and help me," pleaded Asif and helped Mallesh Anna lie down on the ground but his still hands remained tied behind his back and for a moment he thought of untying his hands but again changed his mind.

"Tiwari, please we need to get him out of here."

"Get him out of here? Where do you think you want to take this cave man drug addict?" Tiwari protested

"I don't know but we have to get him out of this place. He is bleeding!" exclaimed, Asif.

"Are you out of your mind?" fumed Tiwari.

"I don't know how we are going to do it but we need to get him out of here. Think of a place where we can shift him," a befuddled Tiwari began scratching his head and mulled for a while. Asif remained silent and waited for his response.

"Alright, I have a place in mind. You know my cousin Raju who stays in Racecourse stables. Let's take him there. But how do we take him there?" Tiwari retorted.

"Don't worry! We will deal with that. Now please wipe his face and carry him outside the graveyard," so saying Asif poured the bottle of whisky on Mallesh Anna's face, Whisky streamed on the ground washing his face and mixing with blood. Tiwari coveted the whisky wasted on washing Mallesh Anna but he had no choice. He was irked to see Asif empty the entire bottle of whisky on Mallesh Anna's face but stood watching silently.

Asif held Mallesh Anna under his arms and looked at Tiwari who stood staring at the wet ground. "C'mon, Tiwari lift his legs." A reluctant Tiwari came forward and lifted Mallesh Anna's legs. They pinioned him and didn't have too much difficulty in lifting him. He was a scraggy man and they had to lay him down only once to open the graveyard gates. They carried him outside the cemetery and kept walking towards Worli naka traffic signals and laid him on the footpath.

It was early dawn and there weren't too many vehicles on the road. They placed him on the footpath and waited for a taxi to arrive. They stood waiting for ten minutes before finally they saw a taxi emerging from Tulsi pipe road. Asif waved at the taxi driver to stop. The taxi driver glanced at Asif and slowed down but the moment he set his eyes upon Mallesh Anna lying on the ground and Tiwari standing beside him he immediately accelerated and raced away. A couple of more empty taxis zoomed without stopping.

It was getting increasingly frustrating; Asif turned to Tiwari and said; "Sit down on the footpath and show as if Mallesh Anna is resting by your side." Tiwari was still reeling with pain and gazed at Mallesh Anna who lay motionless on the ground. He lifted him and placed him beside himself in a position which appeared as if both of them sat together. Tiwari put his arm across Mallesh Anna to hold him inconspicuously and also preventing from falling on the other side.

Asif walked on the road and waited for another taxi to drive by. Soon a taxi approached towards Tulsi Pipe Road. The taxi crossed over but stopped at some distance ahead. Asif walked towards the taxi. The taxi driver was a young man in early twenties who asked, "Where do you want to go?"

Asif was swift to grasp from the taxi driver's accent that the young man was a Maharashtrian and quickly responded in the local Marathi language, "My Uncle got a bit drunk last night and fell down on the road. We have to take him home."

Asif spoke fluent Marathi and the taxi driver did not see any reason to suspect. He smiled and began to reverse the taxi towards Tiwari.

Asif without wasting any time opened the back door, Tiwari got in first and he dragged Mallesh Anna inside but his legs still hung outside the taxi. Asif pushed the legs inside and slammed the door quickly. He came forward and sat next to the driver. The driver kept turning and looking back, Mallesh Anna was stinking of alcohol as a result of the alcohol face wash by Asif. The young driver laughed and turned back addressing Mallesh Anna, "*Kaka,* (uncle) how much did you drink?"

Asif got uncomfortable with his repeatedly turning back and addressing Mallesh Anna and tried to divert his attention by telling him to turn the meter on.

The taxi started and Tiwari realized that there were some flecks of blood on Mallesh Anna's shirt and promptly covered them with his hands. Asif kept the driver busy with his talks. They reached Racecourse in a few minutes and stopped the taxi behind the stables and paid the taxi driver. Tiwari had meticulously held Mallesh Anna by his arms to hide the blood stains on his shirt.

The Racecourse had many green trees, fresh air and was a salubrious place. The ground was wet with morning dew. They placed Mallesh Anna under a tamarind tree, Tiwari walked towards his cousin Raju's home and Asif waited with Mallesh Anna.

Raju was an alcoholic man and a distant relative of Tiwari. He was a tall lanky man in his mid-forties but appeared younger. He was good for nothing, a sluggard who had never worked in his life. He would drink till late hours every night and would continue to do so till morning light.

Asif waited for Tiwari to return under the tamarind tree. In a few minutes Tiwari returned along with Raju. They were acquainted with each other so not many pleasantries were exchanged. Meanwhile Tiwari had already briefed Raju on the way so not too many questions were asked either.

"Raju, we need to hide and nurse this old man for some days," said Asif.

Raju did not bother to ask any questions and was pleased with the fact that Asif would be around for some days and that would take care of his alcohol. He scratched his head and answered, "There is an empty stable behind my house. The racing season is in Pune so most of the stables are empty. We can hide this man over there."

The horse racing season shifted from Bombay to Pune every six months and all the horses would be shifted to Pune too for the racing season. It was a perfect situation, he could not believe his luck and could not have found a better place for Mallesh Anna.

"Let's take him to the Arab line," saying Raju lifted Mallesh Anna and carried him towards the empty stable. It was called Arab line because during the imperial days it was used for keeping a string of Arab horses trained by the British horse trainers. There was a cluster of stables in a row but Raju took them to the stable that was in the farthest corner of the row. They entered the stable and laid Mallesh Anna on dry hay. It was a huge spacious room, the floor was covered with dry hay and had strong odor of horse dung in spite of the fact that there were no horses around.

There was plenty of ventilation in the stable because of a huge wooden window of gothic design. The cool morning breeze hit them. Mallesh Anna's hands remained tied behind his back. He appeared very weak and needed some medical attention. Raju peered at Mallesh Anna with intrigue and wondered, "What on earth would any one gain by nursing or confining a dirty, smelly drug addicted rag picker?" but he did not bother to asking any questions.

Asif removed a few currency notes from his trouser pockets and shoved them into Raju's front shirt pocket. A fifty-rupee note fell on the ground. Raju showed remarkable degree of agility to pick up the note from the ground and put it back in his pocket. He was exulting and drooling by the sight of money and the company he was going to keep for the coming days and weeks.

It was quite bright now and the sun rays crashed throw the wooden windows of the stable. Asif looked at Mallesh Anna's face, the man looked completely emaciated and in a sorry state. Asif felt remorse for him and pleaded, "Tiwari we need to get a doctor." Tiwari peered at his face for a long time. There were mixed emotions inside him. He was peeved with everything that had been happening yet he also secretly admired Asif for his compassion in spite of the fact that he was being audaciously reckless could easily land them in a soup. Yet, their bond of friendship was so strong that he was willing to take that risk for his friend.

"Should we take him to Nair Hospital?" responded Tiwari.

"No we cannot take him to hospital. We need to bring a doctor here."

Tiwari quickly rejoined, "I know Doctor Gohil, he has a clinic in Dhobi Ghat. You know something funny, Doctor Gohil is an amazing doctor who gives his own colorful pills and hardly gives you any prescription for the chemist shop. The last time I went to him for a fever, he asked me which whisky I drank. I answered Desi (country liquor). He immediately suggested I drink 'English' instead." Saying this he started to laugh loudly. Asif was not in a mood for any humor at all yet this funny anecdote brought a smile on his face.

Without wasting anytime they headed straight for doctor Gohil's clinic that was situated near the quaint section of old Dhobi Ghat. They stopped the taxi over the Mahalaxmi Bridge and took the steps down towards the Dhobi Ghat. The morning fish market under the bridge was bustling with people and few dhobis (washermen) could be seen carrying clothes on their backs. They reached doctor Gohil's clinic. It opened at ten a.m. every morning. It was still early morning and they did not know anywhere else to go so they decided to wait right outside his clinic.

The board over the clinic read Dr. Gohil (BUMS). Apparently he was a homeopathy doctor but in a rundown place like Dhobi Ghat it hardly mattered to the local people. It was still early and the shutters were down, some municipality workers were sweeping the roads, the dust was in the air and as a result Asif began to sneeze due to his dust allergy. They kept moving back and forth and loitered around waiting for Doctor Gohil to arrive.

It was ten a.m., most of the shops in the vicinity had opened their shutters and were doing brisk business. The shop next door to the clinic was a glass shop owned by a Bohra Muslim gentleman. The shopkeeper kept moving in and out of the shop and eying them with suspicion. They had been standing outside the clinic for a long time and the shopkeeper was making them more uncomfortable. Tiwari realized that the shopkeeper was being more vigilant and watchful than required and he noticed Asif's uneasy countenance.

Tiwari strode his right leg on the elevated platform in front of the clinic and stared right into the shopkeeper's eyes. The result was instant, the man disappeared inside the shop and stopped his irksome vigilantism. It was half past ten in the morning a few patients had already arrived and left seeing the shutters down.

At last Doctor Gohil arrived at ten forty-five riding his Lambretta scooter. He was a man in his early forties with a receding hairline. He wore a brown T-shirt over black cotton trousers and looked unlike any other conventional medical practitioner. Doctor Gohil glanced at Tiwari and gave him a warm smile and it appeared that they were well acquainted with each other. He parked his scooter right outside his clinic.

"Namaste Tiwariji, how is your malaria? I hope you are not drinking too much," saying he tried to pull the clinic shutters up. Tiwari gave him a lending hand in assisting to open the shutters and responded by remarking playfully, "I have heeded your advice and have been drinking English liquor as you had suggested"

They managed to raise the shutter and all three of them entered the clinic. "Good, good, you must not drink desi liquor, it can make you sick, I am glad that you have heeded my advice and you are drinking English Whisky."

Asif felt it was a highly amusing and comical conversation but his mind was still focused on Mallesh Anna and his bleeding jaw.

Most of the patients lived around Dhobi Ghat and its vicinity, a majority of them were casual laborers, washermen, fishermen or involved in other blue collar jobs.

Doctor Gohil requested them to wait until he attended the patients present inside his cabin. There weren't too many patients so they thought it would not take long but in a couple of minutes a stream of patients started to flow inside the clinic as if by magic and soon there were ten to twelve patients waiting to be examined and more thronged in like bees.

A rather impatient Tiwari went inside to check on Doctor Gohil, "Come in, come in," smiled the doctor. Tiwari signaled Asif to come inside.

"So what happened Tiwari? Who is the patient?" saying he looked at Asif's face through his archaic round spectacles maintaining a stoic countenance.

Tiwari replied, "Doctor Sahib, we got involved in a small accident. We were driving on my bike and we have hit an old drunkard last night and you need to check him." Doctor Gohil pushed his spectacles over his head and without blinking his eyes questioned, "Why didn't you take him to the hospital?"

Tiwari quickly interjected, "Well sir, he was actually drunk and so were we and you know so many questions will be asked so...."

Doctor Gohil did not seem to buy their story yet he did not care or wasn't concerned to know about the authenticity of the story or anything further and he replied, "Okay I will come with you but you see all these patients waiting outside for me? I need to attend to them first."

"Oh sure doctor, we can wait," saying they left the cabin to sit outside, among the patients. The patients were very unusual and appeared very primitive. Dhobi Ghat was one of the most backward areas of Bombay and the patients appeared to be straight out of the book 'Passage to India.'

Doctor Gohil attended his patients at a brisk pace and he would not give more than five minutes for each patient. Amazingly, each time a patient would leave his cabin a new patient would enter the clinic, the flow of patients kept continuing. It was almost two p.m. and it was getting more and more frustrating for them. Finally, at three p.m. the last patient left the clinic and they entered Doctor Gohil's cabin, by the time they were completely exhausted yet miraculously the doctor remained as fresh as he was in the morning.

"So Tiwari, where do we go?" asked doctor Gohil.

"Well, Doctor Sahib, not too far, just here towards Worli Naka." replied Tiwari.

"Oh yes, yes we can surely leave in sometime but let me first have some food." The Doctor placed his Tiffin on the table, they were hungry as wolves but doctor Gohil had a small Tiffin box made of steel with three small chambers, one had cauliflower in it another had dal and last chamber had roti in it. Doctor Gohil gave them a warm smile and invited them to join him for lunch.

Asif thought the Tiffin was not big enough for more than one person and their infringement would not leave any food for him so he politely declined the generous invitation but Tiwari has already taken two steps forward and gnashed his teeth into the roti from the Tiffin. He ate ravenously and had already pounced upon the second roti.

Asif raised his eye brows, in a bid to stop Tiwari from his untenable attack upon Doctor Gohil's Tiffin box and he promptly got the message but there was frustration and dejection on his face. He swallowed the morsel of food which was already inside his mouth and slowly withdrew his steps backwards. Doctor Gohil was either unaffected or was an extra-ordinarily gifted actor because he did not show the slightest displeasure towards the invasion of his Tiffin box.

Asif left the cabin and waited outside. Tiwari followed him, "You should not have jumped inside that Tiffin box." Asif sniggered, "It was just a formal invitation." Tiwari was still licking his lips savoring the taste of whatever food that he had been just prevented from overrunning and replied,

"*Yaar!* We are hungry since morning and did not even have a cup of tea and you Mother Teresa are preventing me from snatching a couple of rotis from Doctor Gohil? I would have died of hunger."

Asif could feel for him and realized that they had indeed not eaten since morning and Tiwari had in fact been injured by the drug addict and was awake the whole night.

After finishing his meal Doctor Gohil walked out of his cabin with his brief case in his hand and flashed his amiable smile. Tiwari rushed forward to carry his brief case for him.

"Doctor Sahib, I will get a taxi for us." Asif humbly offered.

To his astonishment Doctor Gohil answered, "Oh there is no need for any taxi, we can all go on my scooter," saying this he waddled towards his scooter and started to kick start his almost antique Lambretta scooter. Asif was amazed at the modesty of Doctor Gohil. It took at least a dozen kicks for him to get the scooter started. At last it started with a crackle of a noise and was just about the noisiest vehicle on the road.

Doctor Gohil was in the rider's seat Tiwari eagerly jumped behind him and there was some meager space for Asif to hang on to. Soon they were negotiating their way through the traffic towards Mahalaxmi Bridge onwards Worli.

They reached the stables in no time, the place where they had left Mallesh under custody of Raju. The moment they entered the stable Asif was horrified to see Mallesh Anna gagged with a piece of cloth in his mouth and Raju sat drinking whisky next to him.

Asif was flabbergasted, "Raju," what on earth do you think you are doing? Why the hell did you gag this man?"

Raju was taken aback by Asif's outburst and stuttered, "He was screaming. It would have surely drawn attention of someone. What else, should I do?" Asif was still reeling with anger but was greatly mollified with Raju's explanation.

Mallesh Anna lay on the dry grass, his hands bound behind his back and his frothing mouth gagged, he cut out a sorry picture. His eyes were deep and hollow and face was covered with dense beard. He was a very weak old man yet surprisingly he did not have a single grey hair.

Doctor Gohil looked at Mallesh Anna and without asking any questions or seeking any explanations on his injuries started to examine his jaw which had traces of blood. He twisted his head left, right and twisted his face like a bone setter and reached to the conclusion that his jaw was not broken. Asif wondered if the man was either a genius or a quack but he did not possess the luxury of judging him. He was actually glad with the doctor's verdict on Mallesh Anna's injury.

The Doctor gently removed the cloth from Mallesh Anna's frothing mouth and inspecting it looked towards Asif and questioned "Is this man a Gardulla?"

Asif did not volunteer to respond and merely nodded his head in affirmation. Surprisingly Mallesh Anna's eyes remained closed and he did not respond to the doctors prodding.

Doctor Gohil looked up and said, "Boss this man needs drugs and if he does not get his dosage of drugs he will scream in pain. If you want to treat him then you will have to give him cold turkey. It will take a while, some patience and strict regimen for you to get him out of this state."

Asif gazed towards Mallesh Anna's face for a long time and spoke, "Okay, start his treatment right way."

The moment Doctor Gohil heard those words he immediately opened his medical kit and began filling his syringe. Asif looked at Tiwari who had a grimace on his face. He found it hard to digest that Mallesh Anna was now going to be their guest for some more time to come and that Asif had already made up his mind even without consulting him. Peeved, he tried hard to conceal his reproach.

Doctor Gohil gave an injection to Mallesh Anna that resulted in a very low whimper from his lips. Raju remained indifferent to the entire situation and sat on the hay stack with his mind hovering upon his next drinking session.

The Doctor remarkably settled down comfortably on the grass and had no qualms about perching on the filthy ground. Asif wondered if it was modesty or recklessness on the doctor's part. Doctor Gohil got up and spoke while he shut his briefcase, "This man has to be kept tied or he's going to spin out of control again. The patient seems to be a horrible drug addict and soon will be struck by strong withdrawal symptoms. You come to my clinic I will give you some medicines for him." The Doctor gathered his medical kit and padded away towards his scooter. Tiwari followed him silently and sat behind him on the scooter and waited for Asif to join them but he instead walked towards them and said, "Tiwari kindly drop Doctor Sahib and return with the medicine." Tiwari did not react but looked away finding it hard to disguise his discontent. Doctor Gohil miraculously started the scooter in one kick and they disappeared out of the place.

13

Asif returned to the stables only to notice that Raju sat smoking *beedi* on the floor. Asif chided him for sitting and smoking *beedi* on a dry hay stack. Raju recklessly threw the beedi outside the wooden window. He reached for his pocket, "Here is some money. Get some food and give it to him whenever he asks for it. And take good care of him," saying he pushed a few hundred rupees into Raju's front pocket. It brought a huge smile to his face. The money would not only bring food but also take care of his liquor needs for some days.

It was late afternoon Asif returned home and immediately dozed off. When he woke up he realized it was late evening. He quickly washed his face and the moment he stepped out he found Tiwari smiling outside the door. They took a taxi and reached Worli in ten minutes. Tiwari wanted to drink at regular hangout of Poonam Bar but Asif suggested they instead buy some beer from the wine shop. Tiwari didn't mind that option either and also bought some whisky for Raju.

They entered the stables and could see Raju sitting with a half empty glass of whisky and some raw cucumber in a plate along with some chili powder by his side. Raju heard the footsteps and sat attentively. Mallesh Anna was awake and blinked his eyes. He looked completely famished yet he appeared in a far better situation than when they had left him in the morning. Raju spoke, "He was asking for some food so I gave him a *Wada Pav* (Local snack). The moment his stomach was full he began to howl so I gagged him again."

"Did he say something?"

Raju let out a low sigh, "Well, He kept asking for *'maal'*(drugs)"

Asif sat next to Mallesh and spoke to him in a benevolent tone. "Anna, I am here to help you and you have to eat these medicines and you have to stop talking drugs anymore"

He looked into Mallesh Anna's eyes. The man was clearly suffering and Asif couldn't bear to see his pain any more. He had tied, gagged a defenseless, old infirm man and had acted in the most gratuitous manner. He could not bear to suppress his scruples anymore. He mulled and wondered if he had any business to transgress upon the innocent man's life. What moral authority did he have to force him to undergo such trauma?

"Please untie him," said Asif.

There was a hush and no one responded to his command.

"I said, release him," he shouted with a loud voice. Raju was about to move towards Mallesh Anna when Tiwari intervened,

"Are you sure? We have been going through hell for the last twenty-four hours to tame this man and now you want to set him free?" A disillusioned Asif merely kept staring on the floor.

Raju meanwhile had untied Mallesh Anna and removed the gag from his frothing mouth.

Tiwari cautiously asked once again, "Are you sure?"

"Yes! Let him go," answered Asif

Mallesh Anna was completely free and slowly managed to sit cross legged on the ground. Asif beckoned Raju to leave the stables and walked towards the door when he heard the words, "Please give me some water." It was Mallesh Anna.

Asif stopped and signaled Raju to give him water. Mallesh Anna drank water from a brass pot spilling most of the water on his shirt. Asif turned and once again began walking towards the door.

"Wait," mumbled the old man, "Why did you bring me here? You look like a boy from a good family. Why did you get me here?"

Asif turned and sat beside him on the ground. "Anna my name is Asif and I live at Saath Rasta. This is my friend Tiwari and we got you here because I wanted to reform you and get you treated."

"Treat me? Why? Am I related to you? Why are you being so kind to this dirty old drug addict?" asked Mallesh Anna with amazement.

Asif could fathom that in spite of all the years as a recluse and being a miserable drug addict Mallesh Anna was a man of immense grace and spoke with lot of civility and maintained a great deal of acuity.

"Anna, I am really sorry for what we did to you. I found out everything about you. I got to know that once upon a time you were a respected family man and you also owned a prosperous hotel business. You were cheated and destroyed by a man called Sudhakar Shetty. I have to settle a personal score with him and I thought you could help me in my mission".

Mallesh Anna kept blinking his eyes, his countenance changed many folds as he heard Asif's reasoning but was still trying hard to understand the situation. "Son, I am already a dead man and in no position to help myself. What kind of help can this doddering skeleton give you?"

Asif looked into his eyes, "Anna, Sudhakar has not only destroyed you but he is still destroying many other lives." He went onto outpour the painful story of Jenny in the most sonorous manner. Asif went on wiping tears off his eyes as he spoke. Mallesh Anna listened to him attentively without blinking his eyes and did not show any emotion.. Asif spoke like a man in a daze of sorrow. Tiwari walked behind him and placed his hands on his shoulders in a show of solidarity and brotherly affection.

Mallesh Anna was still in discomfort and lot of pain with his injured jaw and drug relapse yet he maintained his composure and emitted fatherly love in his eyes for the young man.

There was a long moment of silence. Asif sat with his head towards the ceiling with a blurred teary vision and after few minutes he lowered his head and looked towards Raju who was so stunned listening to his sorry tale that he did not touch his full glass of whisky and had momentarily lost his penchant for the liquor.

Mallesh Anna kept staring at Asif for a long time without blinking his eye brows. His dreary countenance combined with his painful withdrawal symptoms made him very uncomfortable yet he did not betray his emotion and spoke, "What help do you expect from a dying old drug addict who may not live for too long"?

Asif was full of contrite and lowered his gaze, he did not have the courage to look into Mallesh Anna eyes. He wiped his tears with the back of his palms , stood up and said, "I really don't know Anna; I got to know that you were also a victim of that fiend called Sudhakar and I felt you could help me in some way." He turned towards Raju and said, "Ok Raju, please help Mallesh Anna get out of here."

He looked towards Mallesh Anna and said; "I will give you some money which I hope can compensate a bit for the ordeal that you had to undergo because of me," he said and turned to leave.

"Son, I will have to get back on my feet before I can contribute to you in any way and this old man will do anything to possibly help you. I really don't know if I would be able to help you in any way but I will do my best for you. I was a loser and I gave up so easily. I allowed that guile to destroy me and I have been guilty of procrastination. I have suffered silently all these years and wasted my life. I will try to do whatever I can for you. Please bind my hands and legs and leave the medicine near me or else I will not be able to bear this pain and get treated."

Raju who had so far not exhibited any form of emotions was overwhelmed with Mallesh Anna's words and tears flowed from his eyes. Tiwari who was standing behind Asif burst into tears and hugged Mallesh Anna,

"I am sorry Anna. I hurt you," saying he touched his feet.

It was a very emotional moment and Asif realized it was time to take control of the situation. He brushed his tears away and asked Raju to arrange a charpoy (bed) and blanket for Mallesh Anna and to look after all his needs.

Mallesh Anna was sitting on the floor. Asif bent down and gently pressed his hands in assurance and said, "Don't worry! You will be fine." He left the stables and Mallesh Anna in spite of all his morose and plaintive didn't exhibit much emotion and remained glued to the ground. He got up and without uttering a word just laid down on the charpoy. In all his silence he reflected immense resilience to survive and a commitment to live up to the cause which he was drawn into by a complete stranger.

Asif would visit Mallesh Anna regularly twice a day and oversee his treatment and other needs. Raju was drunk most of the time yet he showed consistent solicitousness towards Mallesh Anna and would bring cooked home food and spend his time around him.

It was seven days into Mallesh Anna's cold turkey. Asif reached the stables at nine p.m. Raju sat listening to All India radio on his transistor. The Hindi film song *'Dil jigar nazar kya hai!'* played in full volume. Seeing Asif, he lowered the radio volume. Mallesh Anna was lying on hay with his eyes closed. It wasn't apparent if he was in a deep sleep or merely lying on the ground. Asif did not want to distract him and beckoned Raju to come out of the stable. A solitary light bulb glowed outside the stables, "Why on earth are you playing the radio so loud?" questioned Raju.

"*Yaar*, old man has been screaming and groaning with pain. I did not want to gag him so instead I raised the volume of the radio to keep his voice down," replied Raju.

"Does he ask for anything? Does he struggle to escape or asks for drugs?"

"Oh No. He does not demand anything nor does he make any effort to escape. He just screams when he is in pain but he has been taking medicine on time," said Raju scratching his head with his left hand and Asif was left full of admiration for the old man's resilience.

It was fifteen days since they had brought Mallesh Anna to the stables from his secret abode, the Jewish cemetery, and he had been taking medicines diligently. His condition was better than the first week. Treatment for drug addiction is never easy and even in the best of hospitals the patients are kept on watch and constantly attended for symptoms as patients can easily escape or turn violent. In case of Mallesh Anna he was not even in a proper hospital or in the most sanitized condition. He would often howl and cry for long hours in pain yet at the same time he showed immense resilience and endured the entire physical trauma just like the Indian mythological snake that had drunk all the poison of the sea.

Raju had been taking care of Mallesh Anna's ministration and as a result he showed remarkable recovery. He no longer needed to be bound by ropes and would go out of the stables for a stroll yet he never left the Racecourse premises and stayed within the enclosures.

Asif arrived at seven p.m. Mallesh Anna sat listening to the radio on hay inside the stable, next to the window on the ground sat Raju drinking whisky in a steel glass, his paraphernalia included a brass utensil of water and some *Jamun* fruit in a brown paper. Both of them did not notice Asif's presence. Mallesh Anna enjoyed the Hindi film song *'Dekha hai pehli baar, saajan ke ankhon me pyar'* on the radio, he sat with his ears very close to radio set even though it was on a high volume and could be heard very loudly. Raju was happiest when he was drinking alcohol and enjoyed every sip of whiskey and savored the blue *Jamun*.

Raju was the first to register Asif's presence and quickly got up and volunteered to get a chair made of cane that was lying outside the stables for him while Mallesh Anna kept swaying his head to the song on the radio. Asif was pleased to see Mallesh Anna in such a jovial mood. The song ended and was followed by some announcements. He switched off the radio and turned his face towards Asif and smiled through his yellow tartar teeth. "I have lost all touch with the present music or songs," he remarked with an impish smile on his face. "I used to listen to Radio Ceylon but these songs are not bad either."

"Yes Anna, these songs are also good," Asif was pleased to see him recover so well.

"Anna, do you wish to eat anything? I can get something for you", said Asif

"I would like to drink some soda," replied Mallesh Anna.

Asif was surprised by the demand of soda and beckoned Raju to fetch soda for Mallesh Anna, Raju immediately responded in great obeisance and left.

That was the only moment when Asif had a private moment with him. The resilience and the determination of the old drug addict, was beyond his comprehension. Mallesh Anna once again started prodding the radio with his fingers. He realized that Mallesh Anna had been wearing the same dirty shirt ever since they had brought him from the graveyard.

"Anna," he said.

Mallesh Anna turned his face towards him and responded with a gentle shake of his head.

"Anna, I think it's time for you to move out of this place, you must clean yourself, shave and start to work." Mallesh Anna did not utter a word and merely shook his head, affirming his acquiescence.

Mallesh Anna looked completely different after he had washed and shaved after many years. He was still an old man but now he looked much younger and civil in this new avatar. A large number of freckles and acnes that had been completely camouflaged under his beard were now made visible.

In a matter of days Asif found a job for him near Tonamec cafeteria outside Grant Medical college hostel building at a Public Telephone or the PCO booth. Mallesh Anna would sit entire day inside the wooden booth and sleep on the quarry bench on the footpath near his PCO booth by the night.

Asif would check on him at least once a day, sometimes early in the morning other times at nine p.m. or when it was time to shut the telephone booth and often he would carry something along with him for him to eat. Mallesh Anna looked healthy and gale and he only got better with every passing day.

14

Ravi Dadhi was not about to easily forget the treatment that he was subjected to and it was only a matter of time before he would seek retribution for his bloody nose.

Asif was not accustomed to the ways of brothel but was pragmatic enough to understand that they had struck Ravi Dadhi a man who would not easily forgive or forget the humiliation. He was apprehensive about Ravi Dadhi's reaction to the drubbing but to his utter surprise, Tiwari was not at all worried or affected about any form of ramification and instead responded by saying, "You don't bother about that pimp. He has enough reasons to fear for his own safety than we do."

Asif persisted with his consternations and said, "But Tiwari, will he swallow the insult?" Tiwari perfunctorily threw the half burnt cigarette away and said, "Look, he does not know about our location. I never give my address to the brothel pimps and in any case if he attempts to act smart we can expose his drug dealings and nail his ass. The pimp makes more money selling drugs than flesh and he won't dare anything thing audacious that would undermine his business. The bastard was a pimp and has only recently graduated to be a drug dealer. Don't worry those pimps are like hyenas inside the brothels but once outside their den they fear being hunted like a dog." And don't forget the bastard has misled us, we have enough reasons to soften him once again.

Asif was encouraged by his words yet he had a lingering fear at the back of his mind and he was aware that a degenerate like Ravi Dadhi was unpredictable and capable of any surprises. Asif's worst fear came true when he launched a cowardly attack on Bablu.

Bablu had visited Kennedy Bridge brothel a couple of times earlier with Tiwari and was unaware of the squabble they had with Ravi Dadhi. Along with few of other pimps Ravi Dadhi had thrashed Bablu and extracted his revenge by attacking a defenseless man, just because he happened to be an accomplice of Tiwari.

Bablu who was oblivious about Ravi Dadhi's bloody nose incident had landed up at Kennedy Bridge brothel drunk one night and was cornered by Ravi Dadhi and his fellow pimp hoodlums. They dragged Bablu out of the room in the middle of his sexual act to an adjoining empty room and beat him black and blue.

An indignant Asif berated Tiwari for not warning Bablu against visiting Kennedy Bridge. He was unaware that Bablu was a regular patron of Kennedy Bridge brothel yet at the same time his conscience didn't absolve him from the guilt of Bablu facing the consequences of his costly slip.

Bablu had no clue why he was badgered by the pimps. In the night when he was facing the kicks and punches he was so drunk that he barely felt any pain but the full brunt of his injuries hit him when he woke up the next morning. He opened his eyes and began hollering in pain.

Tiwari was Bablu's next door neighbor and in the morning he heard the wails and commotions emerging from his neighboring house. Bablu did not tell the real incident to his family and instead concocted a story of having received the injuries in a brawl with unknown people in a bar but in private confided to Tiwari of being bashed up by Ravi Dadhi and his gang of pimps when he had visited Kennedy Bridge brothel to have sex.

Tiwari felt sorry for the severely injured Bablu who had a red welt under his eyes and countless painful broken ribs. He did not reveal to Bablu the real reason why he had been at the receiving end of the pimp's ire at Kennedy Bridge. Asif was also remorseful for Bablu who had unwittingly fallen victim to Ravi Dadhi's fury.

Full of contrite Asif tried to make up by taking Bablu to hospital and got him treated for broken ribs and injuries on head resulting from the pummeling that he had received at Kennedy Bridge. The doctor advised him complete bed rest for a month but it was difficult for a reckless alcoholic like Bablu to stay home and not stray for a long time.

Asif felt it was a moral obligation on his part to help Bablu recover from the trauma and affliction that he had endured. Bablu on his part was happy to receive his daily quota of liquor without working too hard for it. Asif and Tiwari often joined Bablu for his evening drinking bouts till the time he was healthy enough to remove the plaster and support that he used for his broken ribs.

Tiwari remained furious over Ravi Dadhi's assault on Bablu and swore to teach him a lesson but Asif calmed him down and reminded him it would be audacious to tackle Ravi Dadhi at Kennedy Bridge. The creep was not just a pimp but also a drug dealer and paid regular hafta to the local police. Besides it would make matters worse for them if they got embroiled in a personal vengeful duel and lock horns with Ravi Dadhi. Asif did not want another diversion that would create an impediment from his primary purpose that was revenge for Jenny however he remained concerned that Tiwari would end up getting into some kind of tussle with Ravi Dadhi.

Tiwari often had problems with Bablu and did not see eye to eye on many things but he could not tolerate the fact that an innocent Bablu was assaulted by the pimps. Ravi Dadhi had unnecessarily harmed Bablu because he had found a soft target and vented his anger on him just because of his association with Tiwari and Tiwari took it as a personal attack upon him.

Asif feared that Tiwari would be hard to control and may end up getting into some kind of duel in trying to settle score with Ravi Dadhi. He persistently urged him not to indulge in any such revenge at that moment. Tiwari promised him that he would not get involved in an act of retribution without his knowledge and would keep his word yet Asif was not convinced that he would keep his words and not indulge in his turgid bravado.

After recovering from his injuries Bablu stopped visiting Kennedy Bridge but it was hard for him to abjure alcohol, habitual sexual dalliance and his antics after getting drunk. To satisfy his cravings he started visited other cheap brothels around Foras Road and Kamathipura.

It was mere accident that Bablu once spotted Ravi Dadhi at Foras Road. He had not forgotten the beating received at his hands and couldn't miss an opportunity to get back at him. Bablu immediately informed Tiwari about Ravi Dadhi presence at Foras Road. Tiwari warned Bablu against informing Asif about it and quickly began making own designs to settle the scores with Ravi Dadhi.

Tiwari devised a plan to teach Ravi Dadhi a lesson. The plan was to corner Ravi Dadhi whenever he was alone in Foras

Road. Bablu would throw red chili powder on his eyes and the moment Ravi Dadhi would be blinded and squirming in pain Tiwari would smack him hard with his hockey stick and both would make a quick escape after giving him a sound drubbing.

Bablu was nervous about the entire operation and suggested that Tiwari should inform Asif about their plans but the latter had adamantly struck down the idea and convinced him that Asif would not be a party to the idea nor would he allow them to take matters into their own hands hence they should keep him in dark about it. Bablu remained nervous and skeptical of pulling it off but Tiwari was adamant upon seeking revenge and pepped up Bablu every time his desire for revenge got deflated.

Bablu had noticed Ravi Dadhi regularly entering an old building that was situated right at the edge of Foras Road towards Alexandra Cinema. There were no brothels in that section of the building other than some random prostitutes that often stood outside the building. It was not a stronghold of pimps and prostitutes hence to their advantage Ravi Dadhi would not find much support among his tribe if he was attacked at that spot.

One evening armed with chili powder and a hockey stick they decided to extract revenge. They walked towards Alexandra Cinema Hall and waited near the darkest corner of the road near a public lavatory frequented by homosexuals, rag pickers and prostitutes for a quickie. It was a good hideout and a great vantage point because they could watch the entire street yet themselves remained incognito. It was seven o'clock, in the evening still couple of hours to go before the red light area would start buzzing with its nocturnal activities.

Bablu had already emptied half bottle of whisky and Tiwari was two pegs down. Tiwari had hidden the hockey stick inside his shirt, tucked behind his back and as a result walked slowly in a funny manner enduring the discomfort. They waited for thirty minutes before Ravi Dadhi arrived in a taxi from the direction of Nagpada. Tiwari and Bablu were hot on his trail but before they could lay their hands on him he had quickly disappeared into the dark building. They had to back out and abort the plan at the last moment because they didn't know what was in store in the building and could not chase him inside.

Withdrawing back in the unlighted section near the public lavatory they waited for Ravi Dadhi to come out of the building. They remained clueless as to what Ravi Dadhi was doing inside the building. It was certainly not a brothel yet it did not appear to be a residential building either. It was a two floor building that had not been painted for years and had a large terrace overlooking the main road, there was something uncanny and very shady about the edifice.

The traffic passed slowly outside the main road, some Taxis often stopped outside the building. Single nervous men of all ages got down and quickly entered the building and not all of them appeared to be the brothel types. The mystery persisted and an increasingly nervous Bablu wished to abandon the whole task and return home but Tiwari insisted on finishing the job because he wasn't sure if they would get another opportunity to teach Ravi Dadhi a lesson in future.

It had been more than two hours since they arrived at Foras Road. Ravi Dadhi finally emerged out of the building at around nine p.m. scratching his beard. They didn't have much time and thus quickly darted across the road and cornered him outside the building. A drunk Bablu clumsily threw the red chilies into Ravi Dadhi's eyes, some chilly went into his eyes but rest of it flew up in air. Tiwari removed his hockey stick and started raining blows on him. Ravi Dadhi with chilly in his eyes cried out in pain but he was not completely blinded and could see Tiwari, as a result he was able to hold his hockey stick with one hand and begin fighting back. Bablu found the operation getting flubbed and made a quick escape. Tiwari also tried to escape but Ravi Dadhi held on to his hockey stick and began punching him. Tiwari retaliated by punching back and soon it was free for all with both men hitting each other.

A small crowd began to gather outside the building to witness the fight, hearing the commotion some men came out of the building quickly dragging Ravi Dadhi and Tiwari on the first floor and dispersed the crowd that had gathered to watch the duel. Both of them were separated and pulled into a large flat that covered the entire first floor. The doors were locked from outside and it appeared that rooms were shut but in reality the rooms were bustling with activities inside and the locks were only opened every time anyone entered or exited the premises.

Tiwari soon got to know that the building was owned by a small time local don called Khalid Bhai who lived on the second floor. The first floor was an illegal gambling den. Ravi Dadhi had been visiting to supply drugs to one of the gamblers at the club. The club security did not want any commotion outside its premises that would attract police or any untoward attention thus they had promptly ended the tussle by dragging the two men up.

The club was abuzz with the game of *Girdi* (An Indian game of dice) and three card flash but it had all come to an abrupt halt due to the commotion outside the building. A wailing Ravi Dadhi was taken to the bathroom where he washed, cleaned his chilly eyes with water and it instantly helped him to ease the pain and see properly. He was brought back into the main room and he immediately began abusing Tiwari, who wasted no time and abused back.

There was a hush the moment Khalid Bhai entered the room from the terrace. He was a man in his fifties of medium height with eyes that had sunk deep inside due to years of smoking *Ganja*. He was already miffed at the disturbance leading to the stoppage of the games. He walked across towards both the men and slapped them hard across the face and continued to slap every time one of them opened their mouth to complain or explain.

After a brief lull both the trouble makers were made to sit in the center of the room and rest of the men sat in circles around the walls. Khalid Bhai questioned them about why they had created a ruckus under his club. Ravi Dadhi was fast to blame Tiwari for throwing chili powder and attacking him with a hockey stick. Tiwari quickly rejoined narrating the ordeal suffered by his friend Bablu at Kennedy Bridge brothel due to Ravi Dadhi. Khalid Bhai listened to both the sides intently. He felt loathsome when he got to know that Ravi Dadhi was a pimp, but decided to give a fair hearing to both sides.

Khalid Bhai came up with a unique solution. He made both the men sit across each other in the center and others around them like an arena and ordered them to slap each other, one at a time. Whoever prevailed would be the winner. A reluctant Ravi Dadhi wasn't interested in such a contest but was entrapped in the situation and couldn't do much against Khalid Bhai's diktat or dare to antagonize him.

Khalid Bhai converted the entire event into a betting match and began by penning the odds on the winner of the slap fest. Ravi Dadhi was the favorite to win and his rate was eighty rupees to hundred and the odds of hundred and twenty rupees for hundred for Tiwari. There was a flurry of activity in the room and the men in amusement began betting on the two men in the center.

The slapping match started and Ravi Dadhi was the first to slap Tiwari who responded immediately by slapping him harder. After five slaps each, the odds reversed and Tiwari became the favorite. Both continued to thrash the daylight out of other with full force and after the third round, Ravi Dadhi could not take it anymore and holding hands to his ears fell on the ground. The match had ended and Tiwari had won the contest and people who had placed a bet on Tiwari rejoiced and congratulated him.

Khalid Bhai had a great time. He warned both the men to never venture near the club and told his men to first throw Tiwari out of the building followed by a frazzled Ravi Dadhi.

Tiwari made a fast exit. The matter had been settled. Tiwari had endured slaps across his face but he had ultimately won the fight and walked out with immense pride. Ravi Dadhi not only got chilies in his eyes, smacked with a hockey stick but was also knocked out in the slapping match. In fact, he had some strength to fight back and whack Tiwari harder in the slapping contest but had wisely given up the fight prematurely allowing Tiwari to win and was relieved that matters between him and Tiwari had come to an end.

Meanwhile Mallesh Anna had been working diligently at the telephone booth for a month and it was impossible to imagine that he was once a horrible drug addict, but Asif noticed some strange and subtle change in Mallesh Anna's demeanor but was not able to put his finger on it. He would often brush it aside thinking perhaps it was a fragment of his imagination.

The India and Australia one-day cricket match ended at ten p.m. Tiwari stood whistling outside the house. Asif came out of his home and left for Bombay Central's Junction Bar. Tiwari ordered some beer savored the complimentary peanuts and ordered chicken *tikka*. Asif was in no mood to drink and refused. Something rattled at the back of his mind and kept bothering him. It was eleven p.m. and one bottle of beer had already gone down Tiwari's throat and he was lusting for the second. The poet and singer inside Tiwari was just emerging and slowly transcending out but Asif's mind remained focused on Mallesh Anna.

The place was packed with people reeking of all kinds of spirits. The waiter arrived with another green bottle of Sand Piper beer. He could hear a man retch in the wash basin not too far from where they sat. Some men smoked very strong cigarettes in spite of the 'No Smoking' Board loosely hanging on the wall. Other older men sitting on the third table were singing an old Mohammed Rafi song, *'Aye duniya ke rakhwale, sun Dard bhare mere naale'* and most men in the bar were amused by the renditions.

Asif could not get Mallesh Anna out of his mind and was too antsy to continue sitting in the bar and said, "Tiwari, Let's get out of this place."

Tiwari heard him but pretended not to have heard and continued swaying his head to the song and belched at regular intervals.

Asif held Tiwari's hand firmly and said, "We need to go."

"But I have this entire bottle of beer to go?" beseeched Tiwari. He wanted to stay till he finished his beer and palatable chicken tikka on the plate. Seeing, Asif get up, Tiwari made a desperate plea, "Could I have this one…. bottle? Please!" He pleaded with his drunken eyes transfixed on the bottle in front of him.

"Okay grab the bottle, pay the bill and come out," Asif slammed his fist against the table and dashed out of the restaurant.

A reluctant Tiwari kept some money on the table and staggered down the steep wooden steps. The moment they stepped out the security guard tried to hold on to Asif's hand.

"Ok, Boss, Thankyou Boss," He shuddered and indulged in circumlocution for some tips much to Asif's displeasure who was in no mood for such flummery and withdrew his hands firmly. Tiwari in turn behaved liked a born again benevolent and removed a ten rupee note from his pocket and emoted a feeling that he deserved a Nobel prize for his charity. The security guard was at his servile best and it was done with the intent to mock Asif than any genuine obeisance for Tiwari's largesse.

They took a Taxi towards Tonamec cafe. Tiwari kept sipping beer through the way and kept rendering some *shairi (Urdu poetry)* to impress upon the amused taxi driver. The taxi stopped right in front of Mallesh Anna's telephone booth. The booth was closed and Mallesh Anna was nowhere to be seen. His bag was lying on the marble bench but he was missing. There was some beer left in the bottle and Tiwari was focused on savoring the last drop of it. He bought some peanuts from the peanut vendor and stood drinking beer on the footpath.

Asif looked around and cast his eye upon a figure behind the telephone booth. There was considerable darkness behind the telephone booth as street lights could not reach the back of the booth. He saw a shadowy figure behind the booth. He made his way towards the figure of a man who sat completely covered under a black blanket. As he stood in front of the him the man uncovered himself and it was Mallesh Anna. He raised his head and was shocked and astounded to see Asif facing him.

They glared at each other for few seconds. Mallesh Anna lowered his head and slowly pushed the silver foil behind his back and tried to stand on his feet. Asif was disgusted and walked away towards the direction of Haji Ali. Tiwari had been busy with peanut vendor and oblivious to the unpleasant scene of Mallesh Anna being caught using drugs. He watched Asif walk away and realized something had gone horribly wrong. He glanced and saw Mallesh Anna struggling to stand on his feet. Tiwari threw the empty beer bottle on the footpath and rushed towards Asif.

Asif was devastated with the fact that Mallesh Anna had gone back to taking drugs. He had invested so much in the man and had started to look upon him and care for him like a member of his family but he had been let down badly.

Tiwari had to run to catch up with Asif. "What happened? Tell me," he asked gasping for breath.

Asif did not respond and continued to scurry forward with Tiwari trying to catch up.

They reached Heera Panna shopping complex towards Haji Ali circle where cars moved in a circle towards various directions. Asif got inside a subway trying to get to the other side and under the sub way he witnessed some rag pickers smoking brown sugar with silver foil, adding to his disgust and anger.

Asif emerged out of the subway towards the other side of the road. The howling sea wind hit his face. He continued walking for some distance and in all his sullenness sat on the broken depleted concrete block behind the bus stop facing the sea towards Haji Ali Dargah. Tiwari caught up with him and sat beside him, "You shouldn't have wasted your time on that *'Gardulla'*, Saale such creeps never reform. You were dreaming the impossible and sometimes I wonder if you live in the real world." Tiwari went on to lecture him.

A strong whiff of beer hit him every time Tiwari opened his mouth to speak. Asif sat in all his chagrin, he had lost a battle. It had all ended in vain and he had no defense to the flurry verbal onslaught unleashed by Tiwari. In repine he continued staring at the huge sewage gate that disgorged the city waste into the sea. Tiwari persistently admonished him for a long time and after a while Asif had stopped paying attention and got immersed in scheming ways to take on and scupper the guile called Sudhakar Shetty.

Asif glared at the sea as cars kept zooming behind them on the road. Tiwari halted his umbrage and placed his left arm upon Asif's shoulders in a manner they used to do when they would play in their childhood but now they were grown up men. Asif felt a bit awkward yet he knew this was Tiwari's way of showing his support and empathy towards him.

Asif through the corner of his eyes saw a figure standing at some distance behind them next to the bus stop, he turned around only to see Mallesh Anna standing with his head lowered and folded arms. Asif turned his face away in dismay. Tiwari oblivious to Mallesh Anna's presence was glued towards the Sea and the neon signs along with the high rise Usha Kiran apartment. Tiwari turned his face and found Mallesh Anna standing at a distance. He turned himself towards the road on the other side and beckoned Mallesh Anna to come towards them.

Mallesh Anna walked very slowly and was just some feet away from them. Tiwari stepped forward and launched his vituperations at him. Asif did not intervene yet kept a close watch on Tiwari who was gradually inching forward towards Mallesh Anna with his scurrilous tirade. Mallesh Anna stood motionless with his eyes lowered.

Suddenly, Tiwari in a flash raised his hands spitefully and lunged forward to hit Mallesh Anna. Asif threw himself in between the two to stop him from hurting Mallesh Anna and pushed Tiwari away. Tiwari lost his balance and fell on the ground with his upper torso on footpath and lower body on the road. Asif berated him, "Tiwari you have no business to hurt this man. Just leave him alone." Tiwari struggled to get up and dusting his trousers remarked in caustic manner, "I am afraid, I may end up in hospital sooner than this saint," and walked away.

Mallesh Anna stood with his hands folded in a manner of seeking atonement. Asif felt sorry for him, swallowed all his grouse said, "Anna, I have no expectations from you. It's your life. You are free to live it the way you wish," so saying he turned left and started to walk on the promenade towards NSCI club.

The Arabian Sea zephyr on his left and the speeding vehicles on his right kept greeting him as he made his way on the promenade.

Asif noticed Mallesh Anna continued to trudge behind him, he turned back and walked up to him.

"Anna what is it? You are free to do what you want or you can choose the manner in which you wish to live your life." He again turned to leave but stopped and said, "Oh! You want some money, right?" He reached for his trouser pockets but suddenly Mallesh fell on his knees.

"*Beta,* (Son) I am ashamed of myself." It was a momentary lapse on my part. I have been on drugs since years and it's not easy for me to give it up easily, I made a genuine attempt to get rid of the vice and I never had any hope or purpose to live. You gave me a reason to live but I let you down," he paused when his voiced cracked and he continued, "But trust me, I will never return to drugs again. I promise you and I will abjure this habit forever and it will never happen again," saying he lowered his rheumy eyes and fell on the ground.

Asif was embarrassed to see a mortified Mallesh Anna fall on his knees. He quickly helped him get up, "Anna, I will be happy if you do what you just said." Asif hugged him.

Mallesh Anna raised his head looked into Asif's eyes and rubbed his blood shot eyes with back of his palms and without saying anything further turned and walked back towards Tonamec.

Tiwari meanwhile had been watching them silently sitting on the groyne rejoined him scornfully, "Alright my friend, all the best to you in winning this war with the help of a junkie. Everyone is smiling. The drug abuser has been forgiven. Good Luck to you and your drug addict General."

The best thing about Tiwari was that his anger and disappointment was very short lived and it didn't take him long to forget the whole incident and get on with things. Asif put the unfortunate incident of Mallesh Anna's relapse behind him and dutifully persisted with his sincere attempts to help him lead a normal life.

Mallesh Anna had recovered from his momentary relapse to return to a normal life. He would get up early in the morning, clean his PCO booth, go for a walk and then spend rest of the day working at the telephone booth. His telephone booth was busy throughout the day. The medical hostel students would use the booth most of the day calling up their girlfriends or their families. On weekends it would be busy with Racecourse punters and gamblers using the telephone booth for the most part calling their bookies on the illegal black market to place their bets or note down the odds of the black market.

Some of the punters would tip Mallesh Anna generously and that made his life not only busy but fairly comfortable. Asif would spend time with him at his telephone booth usually in the evenings. He would merely sit on the stone bench and talk to him outside the booth or get something to eat for him. Asif also made up his mind that he was not going to take any form of help from the old man and he would face his own battle by taking on Sudhakar Shetty by himself.

He had not for one moment forgotten Sudhakar Shetty. Every time Jenny's face would appear in his mind it was like a spear in his heart. He remained tormented by her memories. He was finding it increasingly difficult to control the smoldering anger inside him at times. He would momentarily try to shrug his melancholy but he knew as long as Sudhakar Shetty lived, it would be impossible for him to breathe easy. It was time to go for the kill.

15

Asif stepped up his mission to obliterate Sudhakar. His first move towards achieving his goal was by getting up early in the morning and surveying Sudhakar's residence, Roopam chambers for a couple of days to study his movements and within days he found out that he was a late riser and would not leave his house before noon. His apartment was a high security building with security guards round the clock on guard. He travelled in a black tinted glass Sumo car. His driver plus body guard was a six feet tall burly, swarthy complexioned man, a native of Padubudri town of Mangalore called Bhaskar. He was a well-built sturdy man with a broad moustache that covered most of his upper lip and would dress in safari suit most of the time. He would leave the top two buttons of his shirt open exposing his dark hairy chest with a shiny yellow gold chain contrasting his skin.

He loved playing with his gold chain most of the time and would keep fidgeting it with his fingers. He would often bite his chain with his heavy tartar teeth or at times simply keep removing his chain out of the shirt and pushing it back again.

Bhaskar would shadow Sudhakar everywhere and Asif soon realized that it was impossible to take on Sudhakar without tackling Bhaskar.

Asif tried to dig out every detail about his past life and found out that Bhaskar was once a local bully and a small time gangster before he became Sudhakar Shetty's personal bodyguard. He had once fired at a top gangster but the man had survived. Bhaskar had been arrested and rival gangster had sworn revenge on him and it was only due to mediation from Sudhakar that the witnesses had turned hostile and a truce was brokered between the surviving gangster and Bhaskar. It was also said that there was some kind of payoff by Sudhakar on behalf of Bhaskar to the rival gang leader to permanently settle the matter and buy peace.

After being chastened Bhaskar remained indebted to his 'Oordar' Sudhakar and had been serving his benefactor loyally. Perhaps it was his safest bet to survive the wrath and the retribution of his surviving rival gangster for his flubbed murder attempt. Bhaskar was a tough cookie and was very likely armed. It was impossible and rather audacious to take on Sudhakar without confronting him. Besides being his driver and bodyguard he also acted as a recovery agent for his boss and would collect bad or defaulted payments from the gamblers that had defaulted on their bets at the club.

Asif followed Sudhakar's trail assiduously. Sudhakar reached his office situated at Navjeevan chambers Tardeo every afternoon around one o' clock. A number of lackeys would be waiting outside his office and below the building near a motor garage that was also owned by him. Thus, Sudhakar's office was heavily fortified with his men all around the building and not a vulnerable place.

Asif followed Sudhakar's black tinted glass Sumo car which was in conformity with criminal elements, on his Bajaj Scooter and at times he came too close to the car. He realized Bhaskar kept a watchful eye through his black aviator sunglasses on any suspicious car or vehicles to ascertain that no hostile or suspicious vehicle came in close proximity. Sudhakar kept opening and closing his car windows at regular intervals to spit the tobacco or *gutka* that he chewed most of the time. The wrappers of Shimla brand *gutka* were routinely thrown out of the running car.

He understood that it was dangerous to get too close to the car, any reckless mistake and he could be exposed. He was just a simple middle class young boy and Sudhakar was a mighty and powerful man who was not only in league with the Hindu but also most of the Muslim gangs of Mumbai. Besides there were also stories circulating that Sudhakar was also affiliated with some Dubai based gangsters.

How would a young man like Asif take on such a powerful man? The only advantage and upper hand that he possessed was the fact that he was a hidden threat and unknown to Sudhakar and could strike at his will but it was imperative that he succeeded in his first attempt. Any botch up or failure could mean a death warrant and the end of him and his first attempt could well end up being his last attempt.

Sudhakar would leave his Navjeevan chambers office around four p.m. for Radio club Colaba every day. It was the largest and among the prominent clubs of Bombay. It was commonly known as a social club but was nothing short of a gambling den for the rich and famous. It was renowned for its high stakes games of cards like rummy and three card flash. Its clientele included top cricket match bookies, race horse bookies, hoteliers and stock brokers along with local councilors among others.

Sudhakar would usually play rummy till seven p.m. at Radio Club and then head for Golden Geese Bar that was owned by him and was like a king in his den surrounded by his servile faithful servants.

Asif assiduously followed Sudhakar's black tinted car from Radio club up to the Golden Geese Bar. Bhaskar stopped the car right outside the huge and spacious Bar gates. Two burly guards in uniform stood outside the massive doors. Sudhakar swaggered inside the gates and the two otherwise arrogant guards stood in complete deference for their master.

It was a crowded locality Asif parked his scooter in an adjoining alley and strutted inside the bar unnoticed. The moment Sudhakar entered the Golden Geese Bar premises, it underwent a complete transformation. The girls started moving to the loud music with greater alacrity. The waiters and managers or captains as they were known flashed their fake oleaginous smiles. Sudhakar's regular customers and acquaintances would greet him with a certain degree of veneration.

The dance bar had two dance floors. The main dance floor was bigger and it was just across the main door. A number of tables and chairs were placed for customers and each table could accommodate up to six customers. The rectangular shaped tables covered with gingham table cloth were made of wood and sunmica. Some had Rexine sofa covers and small glass topped tables. A number of waiters wearing white shirt and black trousers were busy serving and refilling beer to the customers. A few managers wearing black blazers kept a watchful eye on the happenings. They were polite and handled any situation deftly but could easily resort to violence if faced by any untoward situation and would have no qualms bashing up an abusive or a violent customer or any drunkard who misbehaved with any of the dancing girls or the staff. They were fully capable of assaulting or throwing an errant unruly customer out of the bar.

The girls wearing gaudy make up stood on the dance floor in an elevated corner of the room. Asif did not find many of them very attractive, curvaceous or beautiful. The female dancers were dressed in Chania Choli's exposing their midriffs and cleavages through low cut blouses. Most of them were in their twenties while some women were in their early thirties. The drunken customers would place a ten rupee note in between their index and middle finger and would give a gentle nod of their heads to which ever dancer they wished to tip. The dancing girl would sashay across towards the man and collect the money. The girls would at times reward the men by allowing a gentle pat on the derriere or their cheeks and promptly sliding the currency notes into their waiting cleavages. Some girls would do a small jig but most knew very well that more than half of the money would eventually be gulped by the owner of the bar. All the girls would deposit the money in their designated boxes placed in the center of the floor and each box was numbered to know which woman had the highest collection.

There was not much of any real form of dance taking place, the girls would merely sway or at times gyrate their hips to the music. Most girls portrayed their narcissistic self and would constantly observe themselves in the huge glass mirrors facing the dance floor that made the dance floor appear much bigger than it actually was.

Sudhakar would not sit on the front or bigger dance floor room but instead strode directly to the inner room that had a smaller dance floor. Asif did not have any prior experience of visiting a dance bar. He had been privy to stories of dance bars from Tiwari and Bablu but this was his firsthand experience of being inside a dance bar. He sat in one of the empty tables in the front room. The managers and dancing girls immediately noticed his presence and some girls attempted to catch his attention but he found the place abominable. While most of the men enjoyed their beer and were at their prurient best, Asif felt sorry for the girls who had to endure such abasement to earn a living. He failed to appreciate any beauty, attraction or any form of lusciousness and instead wondered if he would ever get an erection sitting in this kind of depressing miasma.

Sudhakar was in the inner room and Asif desperately wanted to get in there. Amazingly the room was sound proof in spite of the loud music being played. He could hear music from the room briefly when the door opened and any one entered or exited the room.

He wasn't sure if he could simply enter the room or it was some kind of exclusive club that had certain protocol. He ordered beer and kept popping peanuts that were on the table along with serviettes in a tall glass. He had no intention of getting drunk or watching the degrading farcical dance. Asif waited for an opportunity to enter the other room. The black blazer captains kept an eye on every customer and one of them noticed that Asif was neither eager to drink beer nor indulge in any kind of prurience towards the dancers. Asif realized that they had eyes on him for a while and he came up with a plan. He directly summoned the manager in black blazer who had been watching him with for a while. The man was awestruck by his confident attitude and quickly began to importune by flashing his unctuous smile

Asif shot at the man, "Look here, I am not enjoying your women or this place. Do you have any beautiful girls or just this three p.m. stuff?" (Three p.m. stuff was a Bombay slang for the left over vegetables unsold in the market which were later in the afternoon sold at throw away price)

The black blazer was impressed by Asif's condescension and answered with the smile "Sir, why don't you get into the VIP room," he said motioning towards the smaller room and ushered Asif towards it. The door leading to the VIP room had a smaller door but it was a compact door like a recording studio with cushions on both sides of the door.

He entered the room and noticed that it had no tables and chairs but cushions and mattresses placed on the floor. The room was not as brightly illuminated as the big room outside and had colorful low power lamps, a crystal ball shed cheerful light on clean tiled floor. There were fewer dancing girls but most girls were in their teens, fairer and prettier than the one outside

Most men in the room were of an average age of forty or above while some of them were in their old sixties. Some of the men noticed his presence as he walked in, but others were busy watching the girls. Sudhakar was sitting in the corner with a couple of elderly men. One of them was in white shirt, white trouser and white turban. The other man was a tall bald man with hollow eyes perched above his cheeks and was perhaps the oldest man in bar.

Two other men sat on the opposite side of the room, one of them had long side burns and a thick gold chain propping through his hairy hoary chest. The man peered at Asif every time he lowered his chin to sip his beer glass.

A couple of subservient black blazers stood in the room but they were a complete antonym to the black blazers of the outer big room and had an amiable demeanor with a friendly respectful smile

Every girl in the room glanced at young Asif and were attracted to him as he was the only young man around but at the same time they were professional enough to know where their bread was being buttered and quickly went back to impress upon the older men.

All the men in the room with the exception of Sudhakar showered the girls with money. Most offered them ten rupees. It had been fifteen minutes since Asif had entered the small room. The black blazers wasted no time to replenish the glasses the moment the beer bottle had been emptied or had any space for more beer in it. Merely drinking beer was not good enough in the small room and one had to be generous in showering the girls with money. Asif needed to boast off or feign largesse conspicuously and beckoned one of the black blazers. He pulled five hundred rupees from his wallet and summoned him to get some change. Within seconds black blazer conjured five bundles of ten rupees each.

The girls kept swaying to Hindi song that went *"Gutoor, Gutoor, Gutoor, Gutoor, Chad gaya oopar re."* A petite girl with whitish complexion kept glancing towards him but he remained focused on Sudhakar. At the same time, he was conscious of playing the game and removed a ten rupee note. The whitish girl without being summoned walked up to him tantalizingly and accepted the money with the most fake coyness one could imagine which was understandably an occupational hazard. He kept raising ten rupees every few minutes and the whitish dancer would walk up to him smiling and tossing her hair back in a seductive fashion. His showoff worked and he was out of the radar of black blazer who got busy with serving drinks to other patrons.

Asif was done with his surveillance of Sudhakar and had discerned that to take on him in his bar would be impossible and suicidal. He felt completely incongruous in that den of vice and wanted to leave and just as he was about to get up he witnessed the Hindi film song *"Choli ke peeche kya hai"* being played on a request by the Sikh gentleman in the white attire. The mood completely changed with girls dancing and swaying suggestively on the floor including the whitish petite girl. Every girl focused towards Sikh gentleman vying for his attention. The Sikh gentleman opened a black leather pouch and removed a bundle of hundred rupees notes from inside. He would give hundred rupees each to any girl whom he pleased and later went to shower his favorite girl with the currency notes. All the men in the room were left bewildered by his munificent exercise of blatant show of money. He had not only displayed his largesse but also humiliated all the other men in the room. Sudhakar watched the spectacle with a sardonic grin on his face.

Asif perceived there was nothing much to scout and his ten rupees notes did not hold a candle to the hundred rupees notes showered by the man in white attire and his naked display of wealth. He found it difficult to breathe by the second under a den of debauchery. He quickly shoved the remaining couple of ten rupees bundle in his pockets and pushed some ten rupees notes in black blazer's hands before making a quick exit. He crossed over to the other side of the road and stood on the footpath patiently waiting for Sudhakar to emerge out.

After waiting for a long time, it was only at one-thirty a.m. that he witnessed the white car with black tinted glass veer towards the main door. Sudhakar walked out and swiftly got on the backseat as the two servile guards closed the door.

The car swerved on the main road towards his Andheri residence and disappeared in the traffic.

Asif trailed Sudhakar for the next two days and was disappointed that he had not found a single unguarded moment but his glimmer of hope arrived on Sunday when Sudhakar left Navjivan society office and instead of going towards Radio Club, his car moved towards Royal Western India Turf club or Racecourse, with Asif hot on the trail pursuing them on his scooter.

The Sumo car romped through the Tardeo Traffic towards Mahalaxmi. The Bombay racing season had commenced. Bhaskar drove the car straight into the huge parking lot that was full of expensive cars and almost all the cars had their chauffeurs waiting inside the cars. The watchmen stood in Khaki uniforms manning the gargantuan iron gates that were a reminiscent of the British imperial architecture.

Asif continued to maintain a healthy distance to Sudhakar's car to avoid getting noticed. Bhaskar stopped the car outside the iron gates and Sudhakar walked inside the gates. Bhaskar maneuvered the car towards the car park, the subservient watchmen expressing their obeisance were too glad to salute the fiend as he entered the main gates. The parking lot outside the member's enclosure was fully occupied hence Bhaskar drove the car towards second enclosure. Asif followed them and quickly parked his scooter in between two cars that did not have a driver waiting or guarding them. One of the other drivers from the opposite side watched Asif from within an expensive Contessa Classic car with certain disdain.

He realized that he could not enter the member's enclosure as it was reserved for the club members only. Asif had to make way towards the first enclosure that was open for general public. He entered the Turf club after buying the tickets that were priced at twenty rupees from the window counter.

He walked inside the Racecourse premises. It was Sunday and the place was packed with people. A number of windows that were known as 'Tote' accepted bets of small punters or the gamblers but the bigger punters and all the movers and shakers did their business in the bookmakers ring that accepted higher bets.

It didn't take long for Asif to understand that bookmakers ring was the most likely place where Sudhakar would be likely found. The place was bustling with people. It was November yet the weather was humid and his shirt was dripping with perspiration. Around fifty temporary wooden structures stood inside the bookmakers ring that demarcated the betting section. Each wooden structure was known as stall and had multiple workers standing on every point like a bunch of grapes in a vineyard.

A fat balding conceiting bookmaker in his fifties, an extremely gaudy and ostentatious character sat on a high wooden chair wearing a Rado watch and gold chain dangling through the vest like the villain of a B-grade Hindi Film. The bookmakers sat on an elevated wooden seat scribbling odds with white chalk on the black board in a hard to decipher hand writing and next to the horse's name, displayed on a paper sheet. There were numerous people inside the bookmakers ring and at times would often trample upon each other due to overcrowding. No one ever complained in spite of being stamped, jostled or pushed by others as most were too busy and engrossed in selecting a horse for the betting in the race, watching the fluctuating odds or glued to the horses being paraded on the paddock or being displayed on the television monitor.

Asif searched all over the bookmakers ring but he could not locate Sudhakar. The third race of the day was just about to commence and commentary was blaring from the loud speakers. People stood glued to the TV that was placed on elevated wooden platforms. When the horses reached four hundred meters to the winning post some of the people started to cheer for their horses loudly. Others shouted calling names of the leading and the favorite horse *"C'mon, Hookah"* others simply *"Hookah."* It was after the race that he realized the name of the winning horse was *Chanukah.*

The race was over and people started to emerge out of the bookmakers ring and dispersed in various other sections of the

Racecourse. Asif felt asphyxiated and could not breathe easily. He had been looking for Sudhakar all over but he could not trace him in that section..

He knew Sudhakar had entered the Members section of the Racecourse but he had a strong feeling that sooner or later Sudhakar would enter the bookmakers ring since he was friends with many of the bookmakers that regularly visited and patronized the Radio club.

The fourth race got over and still there was no sign of Sudhakar yet he did not lose hope and was confident of tracing the man. In the meantime, he decided to check the security of the place and walked all over the place. There were many watchmen or security guards all over the place especially inside the premises near the main gate.

A second gate was exit to the second enclosure, few watchmen with lathis (wooden sticks) stood menacingly at the gate along with policemen armed with double barrel rifles.

The fifth race was about to start in another fifteen minutes and the horses were parading in the paddock. The horses looked well-oiled and magnificent. Tiny jockeys sitting on their backs in their colorful shirts appeared funny. Asif made his way towards the paddock where a huge number of people stood watching the horses; he squeezed himself through the people leading to front and placed his hands on the wooden railings that separated horses from people.

There were at least eight horses in paddock and after taking a few rounds in clockwise manner they began making their way outside. Three horses left the paddock and the fourth was about to leave when his eyes fell upon Sudhakar who stood on the other side of the paddock on the Members enclosure. He was speaking to two other men both of whom had Cole, the race book in hand.

A large number of ostentatiously dressed men and women stood on the lawns of the Members section, most people were aged above thirty. The men were smartly dressed in formal suits, some wore western Homburg hats and women donned elegant saris or western style outfits, some very rich women wore pearl necklaces and fancy hats that he had never witnessed before. A few snobbish men smoked cigars. He spotted Sudhakar standing on the lawns of Members enclosure with his legs apart with the other two men with a touch of paternal contempt for others around him. One of the other men wore a white shirt and khaki trouser. He had eye glasses placed above his forehead and every time he wished to peep into the Cole race book he would lower the glasses to read and push it back on his forehead.

The second man wearing a *Kurta pajama* and every time he spoke he moved his hands in gestures as if to support his rhetoric. All the men primarily appeared middle aged and older. Sudhakar remained glued to the horses in the paddock but at the same time he was also attentive towards the two other men and happenings around him.

The last horse left the paddock and people started entering the bookmakers ring but Asif remained focused on the three men as they meandered through the passage between the two sections manned by security towards the bookmakers ring situated in the second enclosure. Asif was following them closely and was now not more than ten yards behind Sudhakar. There were a number of people inside the bookmaker's ring and at times Sudhakar was rubbing shoulders with others even pushing and jostling other punters in a bid to move forward. He wriggled himself to reach his personal bookmaker. Asif jostled his way closely behind him. Sudhakar reached a particular bookmaker's stall that had a huge sign board painted in black inscribed on top called 'Ram-Shyam and Company.'

The short portly bookmaker was busy wiping the black board with duster and writing fresh odds with chalk. The moment he saw Sudhakar he bent lower and eagerly shook his chalk laced hands with him. Sudhakar meanwhile whispered something in his ears and left the bookmakers ring from rear of the stall. Asif did not know what conversation took place between the two but he could guess that probably Sudhakar had placed some bets at the bookmaker and left.

Asif persistently followed Sudhakar and watched his movements as he along with his other two accomplices crossed over back to the Members section ground. He could sense a window of opportunity and discerned that he could strike inside the race course but his escape would not be easy. He could be easily apprehended as there were a large number of people and armed guards inside the premises yet there was something within him that told him that there was an opportunity.

He continued trailing Sudhakar for rest of the day. There were a total of eight races scheduled for the day after the seventh race got over he saw Sudhakar make his way towards the exit not through the Members enclosure but the second enclosure gate as the exit was closer to his car. Asif rushed towards the Second enclosure gate and reached just in time to see him emerge from it. He looked towards his left. Bhaskar had parked his car two hundred yards from the member's gate.

Surprisingly Bhaskar was nowhere in sight Sudhakar made his way towards the car and Asif followed him from a safe distance. He cursed himself for not having a weapon at that moment as it was a perfect opportunity. Sudhakar reached the car. Bhaskar was lying on the back seat of the car with his legs dangling outside the doors. He quickly sprang on his feet and rushed to open the door and soon the car raced out of the huge iron gates and out of the Turf club premises.

Asif started his scooter but did not bother to trail him any further as he had found his opportunity and now it was not the place but the time he would have to choose to strike. The distance from the enclosure gate exit to the parked car was the only time Sudhakar was the most vulnerable, provided he made that exit earlier as he did that day or else after the last race the parking ground would be swarmed with people making impossible for him to make an easy getaway, if he decides to shoot Sudhakar inside the parking lot.

Asif persisted with his surveillance and went to the Racecourse the next Saturday and learnt that the first race was at one p.m. He reached the Racecourse at noon and waited in the parking lot, some cars were already present while others started rushing in like bees in the beehive. It was ten minutes past one p.m. The first race had already started. He kept watching every car that entered the parking slot but there was no sign of Sudhakar's black tinted glass Sumo.

It was two p.m. and the second race of the day had started. He could hear the commentary that reached outside, he bought some peanuts from a peanut vendor who sold dry peanuts to the waiting chauffeurs. There was very little space for any car apart from some space at the far end of second enclosure, the same spot where Bhaskar had parked his car on the previous occasion.

Finally, at two thirty p.m. he saw Sudhakar's car rumbling towards Members enclosure gate. Sudhakar stepped out of the car and made his way in. Bhaskar turned the car towards second enclosure parking. Asif followed him and realized that he parked at the same spot every time and took off early in the evening to avoid the rush at the parking lot that was generally flooded with people after the last race.

Asif moved in from second enclosure and went towards the paddock, he could see Sudhakar's movements without getting across into Members section. Sudhakar followed the same pattern and stood watching the horses from the elevated stands along with his lackeys and entered the bookmakers ring on few occasions when he wished to place his bets.

Nine races were scheduled for the day with each race stipulated within a thirty-minute gap from the next race. The eighth race ended and Asif wondered if Sudhakar would leave one race early or would stay for all the races. Sudhakar glanced through the Cole book, looked at his watch that glazed over the waning sunlight and made his way towards the exit. Asif followed him outside the gates Sudhakar headed straight towards his car he walked through a number of parked cars and it took him six to seven minutes to reach his car before he made the exit out of the parking space. Asif was now certain that Sudhakar always left Racecourse before the last race and it was great news for him. Attacking him at that time was the safest bet and he immediately began to plan the operation to eliminate him.

16

Asif met Tiwari at Tonamec café around nine pm. Tiwari was already drunk. The moment he saw Asif he hugged him, "Hi where have you been?" with a hint of concern. He was full of brotherly affection yet sometimes Asif would wonder if Tiwari was mawkish and he really meant what he said but inside his heart he didn't mind Tiwari's antics and quirks. He had been a succor in difficult moments in his life. "I am fine *yaar.*" Asif replied and hoped Tiwari would refrain from asking anything more.

Asif kick started his scooter and Tiwari without waiting for any invitation jumped on the pillion seat. They glanced at Mallesh Anna's telephone booth. It was closed and Mallesh Anna missing. He wondered where he had disappeared. In a flash he thought if Mallesh Anna had gone back to taking drugs. It had been a while since they last met.

Asif thought of going to the telephone booth and checking on him but overruled the thought. He gazed at the telephone booth and wondered if he was right in pushing Mallesh Anna to reform and change the course of his life at his age. He had abandoned the idea of taking any help from the old man. It was his battle. He would have to deal with it but he wished from his that heart Mallesh Anna would recover and lead a normal life.

He shrugged his thoughts and raced towards Haji Ali. He parked his bike near the promenade, and both of them as usual sat dangling their legs on the groyne. Meanwhile Tiwari lit his cigarette and blissfully puffed smoke against the fierce sea breeze which threw the smoke back almost as if nature slapping him for the air pollution. A wistful Asif kept glaring at the crashing sea waves before he spoke, "Tiwari, I need a gun."

Tiwari didn't respond and continued to stare at the sea waves almost as if in a deep thought. Asif brooded over his future and wondered perhaps if he was destined to commit a murder and reconciled himself to the fact that it was his lone battle. He had made up his mind. Sudhakar had to pay for his crime. In his turbulent thoughts he also pondered on the ramifications in case he failed in his attempt. The repercussions would be detrimental to him and his future. At the same time, he wondered if he would be able to look at himself in the mirror for rest of his life as long as Sudhakar lived. He would be disturbed every time he heard a name remotely assonating to Jenny or whenever he passed St. Ignatius school and Pinto Undertakers office opposite to it, he would hit rewind mode and all his pain will come back to haunt him. He was not imperturbable and had to take a chance. It was impossible for him to live with the shackles and helpless maudlin of not having avenged the brutality heaped upon his love Jenny.

There was a possibility that if he failed he could probably fall to the bullets of Bhaskar or would be sentenced to a lengthy jail term and with Sudhakar's powerful connections, he would ensure that the jail would be a living hell for him. Yet he could not see Sudhakar go unpunished and live and breathe freely after destroying the love of his life. He was ready to face the consequences.

He looked at Tiwari to notice that he had dozed off; he did not wish to wake him and placed his arms around him to protect him from falling off the cliff. A little while later, Tiwari was awakened from his slumber by a sharp horn of a passing car.

Tiwari slowly opened his eyes to see that he had dozed off on an eight feet high wall facing the sea. The waves lashed on the rocky shores. He looked at Asif's watch. It was forty-five minutes past midnight.

"When did I fall asleep? And why didn't you wake me up?"

Asif decided not to respond to him and instead asked him the same question that he had earlier.

"Tiwari, I need a gun. Can you arrange one for me?"

Tiwari rubbed his eyes, "Gun! *Haan*? You want to shoot that dog?"

Asif again chose not to respond to him and instead asked him one more time,

"Can you get a gun for me?"

Tiwari withdrew his legs from the direction of the sea and now turned towards the road, mulled for a minute and replied, "I think I can try. Let me talk to Dig."

Dig was a friend of Tiwari and was of the same age.

"You think Dig can help?" asked Asif.

"I think so. He has some connections in infamous Pathari Chawl and had once brandished a pistol during a brawl to impress some dancers and manager at Chandra Bar."

Asif had a week ahead of him before he could strike at Sudhakar and needed to get the act together. Dig lived in the notorious Pathari Chawl near Byculla. He was friendly towards

Tiwari. They had spent time together in numerous drinking binges in shady restaurants and bars.

Asif was never too fond of Dig, though he never despised him either. Dig was born a Hindu. He was orphaned at a tender age after losing his parents. He was adopted by a Muslim family. The name Dig was a common Marathi language sobriquet labeled upon him because of his dark complexion.

It was not clear if Dig was a part of Pathari chawl criminal gang but he was certainly acquainted with some of the members of gang that lived in the Chawl. Tiwari felt he was the right man for the job and could be useful in arranging the gun.

The ten days of Navaratri Festival of Goddess Durga were in full fervor, Pathari chawl was well known for its annual Navaratri celebrations. Contrary to the local tradition, usually it was the Ganeshotsav that was widely celebrated in Maharashtrian areas and Navratri was restricted to Gujarati localities of Bombay yet Pathari chawl in spite of the overwhelming Maharashtrian populace had the distinction of holding a grand Navaratri Celebration.

It was midnight, yet there were many people on the streets on account of the Navaratri Festival. Asif preferred to walk rather than use his scooter. They made their way towards Pathari chawl with a stream of people headed in that direction. A small pandal (stage) stood outside the transit camp building, some people from the chawls danced with rag tag wooden sticks on *Dandiya Ras* (Folk music) music. Abridged bamboo sticks were converted into *Dandiya*. People of the slums danced to the standard Gujarati *Dandiya* medley being played on loud speaker.

They stood watching them play for ten minutes before proceeding towards the Pathari Chawl. Asif had never stepped inside the notorious Pathari chawl. Tiwari had been there on a few occasions. The local don who was locally known as 'Papa' belonged to Pathari Chawl and ran his fiefdom within the confines of the chawls.

At the moment Papa was in prison but the place was constantly under police surveillance because the don's family and his henchmen were still inside the Chawl. Some of the boys of Pathari chawl stood outside the massive iron gates that greeted the visitors at the chawl. The boys typically wore shorts and some elderly men wore a white kurta pajama with a *tilak* (Hindu religious Symbol) on their forehead.

Asif was nervous and momentarily wondered if it was the right moment to enter the Pathari chawl but Tiwari felt it was the most appropriate time to mingle among the devotees streaming in and out for *Darshan* without raising any suspicion.

A large number of people stood outside the massive iron gates. The gates were never fully opened anytime of the year except for the Navaratri festivities. The rest of the year the inhabitants of the chawl would enter from a small window at the iron door that was only large enough for one individual to enter or exit at a time. But because of Navaratri festivities the huge iron gates were fully opened for public.

Asif stood outside the chawl and watched a huge queue of people stream in and out of the chawl. A large number of boys and some of them henchmen of Papa gang stood on vigil outside the gates. Along with them also stood a large number of plain clothes policemen closely monitoring the movement of people going in and out.

The local boys and the policemen played 'chicken' with each other. Tiwari spotted Ganya outside the gate. Though Ganya lived near Shakti Mills compound he had many friends and was well acquainted with most residents and members of Papa gang inside Pathari chawl, thus making it easier for him to move in and out of the chawl. Ganya helped them enter the Pathari chawl premises bypassing the long queue of devotees.

Loud speakers played devotional songs in praise of the Goddess *Durga* on high volume. The place was brightly lit up with numerous halogen lights. They pushed their way towards the stage where the idol of Goddess was placed. Tiwari asked him to wait near the stage as he left along with Ganya to fetch Dig. Asif looked at the large number of devotees that had turned up for *Darshan* in spite of the ill repute of the place. The only difference was that there was no *Dandiya* being played or film songs on loud speaker. People offered their prayers, made obeisance and left.

It was one a.m. and people still continued streaming in. A number of local boys also looked at him suspiciously for standing aimlessly near the stage. Soon he saw Tiwari emerge out of the crowd along with Dig.

Dig squinted at him through his drooping eyes. Asif smiled at him. Tiwari spoke,

"Our handsome man had slept early tonight."

"Hello Dig! I have some important business with you."

Dig was still rubbing his eyes.

"Dig I need a gun for a few days."

Upon hearing these words Dig stopped rubbing his eyes and raised his eyebrows,

"Need a gun? Why?"

Before Asif could respond Tiwari interjected,

"*Array Yaar*, he wants to give some *Dhos* (intimidate) to some *Lukha* (Bum)."

Dig suddenly realized his moment of importance and responded haughtily trying to hog all the attention.

"I don't have a gun with me," he replied wryly.

A gloom transcended upon Asif's face and he did not know how to react to the situation but Tiwari knew Dig better and immediately reacted by throwing a challenge at him.

"Oh! C'mon! Dig, I had high expectation from you and bragged about all your connections to Asif but you turned out to be a real dud a *phuska* bomb (damp squib)."

These words were enough to provoke Dig who quickly responded to salvage his pride

"Oh! Don't worry, I may not possess one but I can arrange a *Ghoda* (Gun) for you."

Asif could see that Tiwari's trick had worked.

"Ok, we shall meet you tomorrow afternoon at two p.m. under the railway bridge warehouse." He shook hands and quickly disappeared in the crowd of devotees. The reason for his quick exit was that Asif did not wish to be in a capricious situation once again and deny further opportunity to Dig to further gloat over his moment of importance.

Outside the gate people kept streaming in and out of the iron gates for *Darshan*. The plain clothes policemen were exhausted and retired by now, only the local Pathari chawl boys stood outside the gates.

Asif had always dealt with Dig in contemptuous manner. It was a great moment for the latter who felt special for having been pivotal to the meeting. After all, he was doing a favor to Asif. The warehouse was on the east side of the railway bridge. Asif reached on time along with Tiwari. Dig was already present under the scorching sun wearing a funny sleeveless red T-shirt. The moment he saw them he flashed a huge smile, his spotless white teeth gleamed in contrast to his dusky complexion.

"I don't have much time," started Dig in a rather garrulous manner perhaps still trying to gloat over the fact that he was made to feel significant. There was not a soul around. Dig removed revolver from his back pocket. "This is a foreign made rifle," he gloated displaying his sparkling teeth.

Asif wondered what kind of a cretin Dig was who called a revolver a rifle. However, he did not make any attempt to educate or embarrass him.

He held the gun in his hands and realized that it was heavier than he had anticipated,

"So I just pull the trigger, that's it?"

"Oh yes, just pull the trigger and Boom," Dig acted as though firing through the tip of his fingers.

Dig handled the gun in a scrupulous manner and Tiwari made him believe that they were going to merely scare someone with the gun and there was no real intention to cause any serious harm.

Dig was at his credulous best. He never imagined a guy like Asif would ever be malignant towards anyone yet when Asif questioned about the trigger there was a sense of portentousness in his voice. Continuing his garrulous banter, he asked, "When are you going to return the gun?"

Tiwari quickly jumped in, "You will get the gun by Monday," and tried his best to mitigate Dig's fears.

Asif locked the gun and kept in a plastic polythene bag that he was carrying.

"How much do I pay for this?" asked Asif earnestly. Tiwari again quickly jumped in. "Oh C'mon, Asif you should go home while Dig and me discuss the rest of the stuff over drinks," saying he gently prodded Asif on his shoulders signaling him to leave.

A bemused Dig was left nonplussed, Tiwari had been deliberately trying to downplay the significance of the event and sounding rather facetious to suppress the magnanimity of the situation.

Asif met Tiwari at six p.m. An amused Tiwari could not stop laughing. "Boy, I tell you, you should have seen Dig's face." Asif responded with a smile, "How much do I pay him?"

Tiwari replied, "Two thousand rupees but only if you are alive." This time they both burst into laughter.

It was three more days to go before the Sunday races and his final encounter with Sudhakar. Asif's heart kept pounding every moment with piercing trauma through his chest and at times he wondered if he would survive the pressure or just collapse and suffer a heart attack. Dying of a heart attack would be a shame and a terribly undignified death. He did not mind dying taking a bullet instead. He took a deep breath. The image of Jenny appeared in his mind and along with it he would be reminded of the bestiality she suffered and of the miasma of the brothel feeding his hunger for retribution and in a way giving him strength to pursue his mission.

Tiwari who had been extremely facetious and constantly attempting to disparage the whole issue all the while knowingly ignoring the gravity of the situation turned saturnine as the days drew closer. Finally, it was Saturday. Just one more day to go before Asif would carry out his plan. Tiwari stood whistling outside his door. It was a peculiar whistle that was not loud rather feeble similar to the shrilling sound of a milk cooker just loud enough to be heard by the person intended.

He wasn't as shabby as usual but surprisingly rather well dressed and sober for a change. Opening the door Asif acknowledged him and walked towards him by nodding his head and also prompted him to stop whistling. Inadvertently they began walking towards Babu Bhai's restaurant. The restaurant was as usual busy with its morning hustle bustle. Babu Bhai smiled on seeing them and was about to say something but restrained the words in his mouth at the last minute. Perhaps even he sensed from their body language that something was unusual about the day. He merely smiled and was back to his business of collecting money and interacting with the waiters.

The waiter brought two cups of *Paani kam chai* (special tea) for them. Both of them drank the tea rather quickly and ordered another couple of cups. The second round of tea was much slower than the first. Asif remained mute and Tiwari had not uttered a word so far. Twice he was on the verge of speaking but had decided against it. At last he mustered courage and held Asif's wrist gently, "Asif do you think it's worth it? You think you will get away with it after shooting him? He could be armed, and you know his bull dog Sudhakar is surely armed." He maintained holding Asif's wrist, paused for a moment and spoke again, "And what if you are caught by the bystanders or if someone decides to become a hero?"

Asif with his eyes on the table listened patiently and did not interrupt Tiwari who continued to persuade him with his reasoning for a while before stopping to sip from his cup. The silence would last for few seconds and before he could start again Asif looked into Tiwari's eyes and said, "Don't worry I will finish the job and escape. In case I fail I would rather pull the trigger on myself than reveal your or Dig's name." Tiwari got agitated and tried to interrupt but this time Asif pressed his right shoulder gently with his hand in the sign of assurance. Tiwari got convinced that Asif had made up his mind and it was not easy to getting to change his mind, perhaps it was irreversible.

He did not argue any further and reconciled with the fact that Asif was determined to go ahead and murder Sudhakar and face whatever consequences that may lead to. It was rather ingénue or deliberate oversight that he ignored the scenario where Asif could be arrested and the trail would lead up to him. The bond of friendship was very strong between them and Tiwari was ready to own up and face any unfortunate eventuality or turn of events as a consequence in case things go bad and that would be his own contribution as a friend.

Though it was Asif who was going to pull the trigger yet Tiwari was fully ready for the repercussions. He had come this far for Asif and he would go the extra mile. It was in a sense a good cause. People like Sudhakar deserved death and nothing less. Yes, there was a law and yes there was a little thing called money which played a massive role in the delivery of justice. Both Asif and Tiwari knew it, and that is what gave their cause a seal of approval.

Asif had never used a revolver in his life. There were six bullets ready to be fired inside the revolver but he needed to make sure that he would not end up committing some blunder and he felt it would be safer to try using the revolver once. It was difficult in a highly populated city like Bombay to fire a gun without getting noticed. He thought of a place where he could fire the gun and not get noticed and there was only one place that would be the safest which was the middle of the Polo ground.

The Polo ground was like an oasis in the city, a large piece of verdant land with empty grassland in the center and surrounded by a large ground which was sparsely used anytime other than when Polo matches were played in adjoining ground. It was only in the evening that few joggers and horse riders would come for practice. In the afternoon it was usually empty.

Asif removed the revolver from the polythene bag; tucking the revolver in his trousers he let the shirt lose covering it. It was a rather humid. The heat was at its peak. He reached the Polo ground by jumping over a few white picket fences. The usually tall grass on the periphery of the ground had been recently mowed. But the middle of the ground was still dense with tall grasses. He noticed some grass cutting laborers at a distance but they were a decent distance to notice his gun, yet he wasn't sure how much noise would be created by the firing of bullets and if that would attract attention of the laborers. He walked ahead to the center of the ground and found a huge open sewage passing through the ground. One had to go below the ground to reach the flowing water levels. It was a perfect place that kept him away from the sight of the workers. The low ground would also reduce the noise resulting out of the firing of the gun.

Asif jumped down and could see the sewage water passing beneath. It was the gutter flowing towards the Arabian Sea and the stench filled his nostrils as he battled the nauseating feeling. He removed the handkerchief from the back of his trouser pocket to cover his nose and while doing so accidently dropped the revolver on the ground. It fell on the ground and slipped towards the sewage but to his good fortune rested just next to the flowing dirty water. He quickly jumped down to pick up the gun and had a closer look at it. To his good luck it had not been affected by the fall. He opened the revolver and did what Dig had demonstrated earlier. He opened the cartridge and checked the bullets; all six of them were intact. He got a faint smile on his face wondering how on earth did Dig buy their cock and bull story and in fact did not even bother to remove the bullets. He aimed the gun at the iron rods placed next to the sewage and pulled the trigger. The bullet hit the iron rods and flew inside the gutter splashing some water.

His throat was parched and his shirt was wet with perspiration due to the heat and the nervousness. Yet he heaved a sigh of relief for successful operation of the gun. Out of the six bullets he had lost one but he felt more confident, it gave him a huge boost in firing the gun. He locked the gun and quickly tucked it back under his shirt and emerged out on the open ground. His shoes were besmirched with mud. He wiped his sweating face with handkerchief, emerged from the pit and peeked at the laborers. They were no longer standing in the sweltering sun but by then they had all dispersed under the umbrellas to eat their afternoon meal. To Asif's relief no one had heard or noticed the firing of the gun.

17

Sunday:

Asif knew in his heart that his moment of reckoning had arrived. It was the day Sudhakar would be attending the races at the Racecourse. Asif had already got a Cole race book that gave the time table for the day's races. The first race was scheduled for one pm. Sudhakar would usually arrive after first race. To be on the safe side of any unforeseen eventuality Asif had to be present at the parking lot well in advance.

He woke up early in the morning and checked his revolver many times. It was the day; he had been waiting for. There would be no second chance. It was a do or die for him.

It was nine a.m. in the morning and he made his way towards the Haines road cemetery. Being Sunday, many people turned up at the burial ground to pay obeisance to their loved ones who were buried in the cemetery after the Sunday mass. An elderly couple was busy cleaning the grave of their deceased loved one. Few others stood beside a freshly erected grave on the left corner of the graveyard with flowers in their hands. Asif walked towards Jenny's grave. It was one of the most unadorned graves in the entire graveyard. A bland cross stood on the ground with an epitaph that could barely read her name, date of birth and death.

He picked up and cleaned a few dry leaves and grass that covered the grave and brushed them aside. He realized he had not brought any flowers or a wreath to be placed on the grave. Remorsefully he looked around and found wild red flowers in the burial ground. He plucked few red unknown wild flowers. They reminded him of the red rose he had presented to Jenny as a schoolboy, bringing back spasms of traumatic memories back to his mind. He gently placed the flowers on top of the grave.

It was a solemn moment for him as he sat by the grave with his eyes shut saying a silent prayer for the departed soul of the girl he loved so much. He promised her that he would punish her tormentor come what may. There were no tears in his eyes and he was firm in his resolution. He needed to preserve all his anger. It gave him the strength and motivation to stay strong and to pursue his vendetta till he achieved his revenge.

Leaving the cemetery, he headed straight for the Racecourse. It was eleven a.m., still a couple of hours away from the start of the first race. He parked his scooter inside the parking premises removed the number plate from the back of the scooter and disfigured the front number plate. He slowly made his way towards Babu Bhai's restaurant.

He sat on his regular corner table and ordered tea. Before the tea arrived he noticed Tiwari entering the restaurant heading straight towards his direction. "Where have you been? I have been looking for you since morning," he asked.

Asif did not respond to him but signaled the waiter to get another cup of tea. The waiter soon arrived with two cups of tea. Tiwari sat on the table and continued to attempt caution to him about the consequences of his plans in spite of the waiter's presence. Asif poured the tea in a saucer and began sipping it in a typical Indian style. Tiwari stopped speaking as his attention was diverted towards the tea cup on the table. It was a moment of silence and the only sound that could be heard was of Tiwari slurping the tea from the saucer.

Tiwari stopped his discourse and appeared to have accepted the situation and finally gave in to Asif's irrevocable resolve and conviction to go ahead with his objective. They walked out of the restaurant. Asif did not wish to get weak in his resolve or oscillate his determination by getting involved in any sort of emotional interaction with his best friend as he knew Tiwari was sentimental and capable of an emotional outburst. Tiwari hugged him and wanted to say something but Asif stolidly controlled his emotions and did not reciprocate further. Maintaining his firm visage, he said, "I will join you for a beer in the evening," and headed straight towards the Turf club parking lot. Tiwari stood on the road and watched Asif walk away.

Asif could have made an attempt on Sudhakar's life while he entered the parking lot but it would have been a far dangerous proposition with the high number of policemen and security guards present at duty at start of the races. Contrary to that in the evening the security would be negligible as the security guards and the policemen would be exhausted at the end of their duty.

Asif looked at his watch. It was half past twelve, thirty minutes before the first race would commence but the cars had already had begun to arrive in the parking space. He raised his head to gaze at top of the Turf club. Numerous colored flags stood fluttering on the top, a practice that had been on since the British days. Within no time the entire ground was swarmed by cars. The enclosure towards Wellington club was full of swanky, expensive cars while the eastern section consisted of cars such as Fiat, Ambassador and yellow and black taxis. He had never worn a helmet but he bought a new helmet some days back and fitted it on the side of the scooter. The plan was to wear a dark helmet and ride the scooter right up to Sudhakar, pump bullets into him and make a quick escape from the spot. He had already parked his scooter near the main exit.

But for that to happen as smoothly as planned he would have to have a perfect timing. It would take approximately two minutes for Sudhakar to exit the gate and reach his parked car in the parking premises. And it was the gap between his walk from the gate up to the car that he needed to strike. If he got too late he could face retaliatory fire from Bhaskar and it was also important that he would have a smooth scooter ride till the point where he would use the gun and make a clean getaway.

It was a huge parking lot and there was every possibility of his way being blocked by a random vehicle anywhere at the start or end of his ride inside it. Moreover, there were a large number of people present in the parking lot which could result being an impediment to his plan. He made his way towards the Wellington club entrance gate where most of the cars entered and by now most of the parking lot was already covered with cars. It was twelve forty-five p.m., fifteen minutes before the first race would start. He could hear the announcements from the loudspeakers in the parking lot. His mind was focused on the announcement but at the same time stood awestruck and enamored by the vintage Rolls Royce when he noticed Sudhakar's car entering the parking lot. He walked briskly behind the car. His heart sank because Sudhakar was earlier than expected and instead of parking his car in the furthest corner. Bhaskar parked the car much closer to the entrance gate which meant he had far less time than he had planned. The situation had changed and now he would need approximately one and a half minute to complete the job. It was an ominous sign. He watched from a distance standing behind a Maruti car Bhaskar wearing aviator sun glasses emerge from the car and open the door for Sudhakar who rushed towards the Turf club gates after listening to the music on the loudspeaker announcing the stalling of horse for the first race.

Sudhakar who wore a short cream colored kurta over black trousers entered the members enclosure. Asif bought the entry tickets and quickly entered the first enclosure. The moment he entered the Turf club he could hear the announcements on the speaker of completion of the stalling of the horses in their gates. Soon the race started and the commentary resounded from the loudspeakers. Some people rushed on the stands to watch the race while others were content watching it on the television set situated all over the premises. There was a roar of the crowd as the horses reached the last stretch towards the winning post and a louder roar followed when the name of the winning horse was announced.

Asif made his way towards the paddocks and stood by the side of white picket fences that separated the first enclosure from the Members enclosure. It was the best vantage point to observe Sudhakar entering and exiting both sections of the ground. It was an unusually hot and humid day and being Sunday the ground was packed to capacity with hundreds of people but that also exposed him to a danger of missing Sudhakar among the throngs of people on the ground. He was not concerned much about losing sight of him in the ground but it was more important that he would not lose him at the time of exiting the Turf club gates.

Asif kept an eye on Sudhakar and watched him enter bookmakers ring to place his bets along with his lackeys and return back to the Members section. He ardently tailed him in spite of the humidity and as the day progressed it only got worse. His shirt was soaked with perspiration with his sweat dripping from his forehead down to his cheeks.

The Racecourse premise was full of people, from the hardcore gamblers of the first enclosure section to the snobbish horse owners and pretty women of the Members section. Most people were busy with themselves and didn't care what the others did and most of the time they were either glued to the horses or peeping into the Cole race book. Asif continued to follow Sudhakar as the day progressed fast, it was four p.m. and the last race was scheduled for five pm and as a regular practice Sudhakar would leave the Racecourse after the second last race. That meant he would be leaving the Racecourse around four thirty pm.

Asif tracked him closely with a constant eye and it was imperative not to lose sight of him as the moment drew near. It was the eighth and the second last race, Sudhakar entered the bookmakers ring which was packed with people. He jostled his way towards his bookmaker and after placing bets, instead of moving towards the exit in a sudden turn of caprice stood listening to the race commentary and watched the race on TV monitor just outside the bookmakers ring.

Asif was flummoxed by the sudden unexpected turn of events. He had planned to rush outside just before Sudhakar start his scooter and attack him as he made his way towards his car but to his dismay Sudhakar had not made his way out in spite of the second last race and chose to stay back. The race started and the horses bolted out of the gates. He closely watched Sudhakar glued to the TV monitor watching the race. The race concluded with a huge cry among the punters but the moment commentator announced that the winner was yet to be announced as there was a close photo finish between two horses for the first place, there was a complete hush on the ground.

People waited with bated breath for the results of the photo finish to be announced. Sudhakar also waited anxiously for the announcement of the winner. The winner was announced; it was a horse named Clarions Glory which was the horse of the season. Sudhakar appeared dejected hearing the result and removed his handkerchief to wipe his face. Asif moved towards the gate to take lead but to his utter disbelief instead of moving out Sudhakar headed back inside the Racecourse.

It was a highly unusual move and it appeared as if Sudhakar had lost a lot of money in the second last race and had decided to return to bet in the last race to recover his losses or there was likelihood that he had a tip for the last race. This was bad news for Asif. If Sudhakar left the race after the last race it would lead to a huge rush of patrons in the parking ground and that would make his task precariously dangerous and his getaway tougher. He did not have an option of aborting the mission as it would not be easy to sustain his momentum and he also had to return the revolver to Dig, hence he decided to pursue his irrevocable resolve irrespective of its ramifications.

He made up his mind that he was going to commit murder that day come what may and he went back to shadowing Sudhakar and stood watching the man near the paddock. To make matters worse he met Sanju who was surprised to see him inside Racecourse. Sanju shot a volley of questions about his presence at the Racecourse and horse racing. Asif answered him politely but was getting annoyed at being distracted in his pursuit. He got rid of Sanju after displaying immense patience. Sudhakar stood smoking a cigarette, insouciantly blowing smoke in the air even after apparent disappointment of losing in the previous race. It was the last race. The horses left the paddock towards the starting gate. The same ritual was repeated, Sudhakar walked inside the bookmakers ring but this time after placing his bets did not watch the TV behind the stalls and in sudden turn of events instead began walking towards the exit gate and stood near the edge of the gates listening to the commentary.

Asif had not anticipated this scenario. Apparently Sudhakar's move was prompted by his decision to hear the race commentary and the results and quickly leave as the race concluded to avoid the post-race rush. Asif had to react quickly to the new development and tried to work the situation to his advantage. He left the Racecourse exit before Sudhakar and quickly rushed outside the gates towards his scooter.

He could observe Sudhakar listen to the commentary of the last race standing on the edge of the exit gate. Asif used the opportunity to rapidly wear his helmet and prepare for the assault. He groped his revolver inside the shirt and started the scooter. He continued to race the accelerator to keep its engine on and save some time but soon realized that his idea of starting the scooter early was not the best one. It was humid and his racing of accelerator led to sweating of his hands yet he could do nothing about it.

The last race had commenced and he could hear the commentary outside the gates. He quickly removed the helmet to wipe the dripping perspiration from his eyes with one hand and wore his helmet back, at the same time pushing the accelerator with the other hand. The race concluded and there was again a roar from the crowd. He saw an exultant Sudhakar pump his fist in the air to celebrate the winning of his horse. As he was already at the gate he quickly made his way outside the gate and was among the first to dart out of the Turf club.

Asif quickly raced his scooter in his direction. He glanced towards Bhaskar and found him standing outside the car and waiting for Sudhakar. Asif had less than a minute to finish his task and his heart thundered under his chest. Some people started to trickle out of the Turf club without waiting for results to be announced. Asif's throat parched with anxiety and his shirt soaked with perspiration. An exultant Sudhakar emerged out of the gate with a satisfied grin on his face. Asif raced his scooter in Sudhakar's direction and was fifty yards from his target. He pushed his hand inside his shirt to remove the revolver but to his utter surprise he noticed Sudhakar suddenly slump on the ground with a loud cry. Bewildered he looked around to see what had happened. Some people rushed in different directions others came forward to watch the commotion and so did Bhaskar who had been watching from his car.

Asif had one hand grasping the hilt of the loaded gun and fingers on the trigger under his shirt but when he saw Sudhakar crash on the ground he promptly pushed back his gun and rushed forward towards Sudhakar. The man was groaning in pain and his face turned into a grisly macabre with Mallesh Anna standing next to him with a green bottle of acid in his hands. Bhaskar rushed forward removed the pistol and shot Mallesh Anna in stomach at point blank range. Asif tried to pull his gun to shoot Bhaskar but Mallesh Anna before falling on the ground had managed to throw the remaining acid on Bhaskar sending him reeling and cowering on the ground because of the effects of acid burning his face badly.

Asif pushed his gun back inside his shirt. A crowd began to gather at the scene to see what was going on and some of those who had watched the incident began to escape in mad frenzy fearing for their own lives. Sudhakar stopped groaning. Only his legs moved in pain. Bhaskar had shot Mallesh Anna more than once but he was also critically injured by the acid thrown across his face and as a result he tried to run outside the main gate writhing in pain but crashed on the ground.

Mallesh Anna lay on the ground with flecks of blood emerging from his mouth. Asif removed his helmet and walked past Sudhakar, his face had turned into a grotesque piece of charred meat. Mallesh Anna was breathing his last yet he had an immense sense of fulfillment on his face. He had a faint smile on his lips and fatherly love in his slanting eyes.

Asif never understood what had happened. Perhaps Mallesh Anna had been watching him and his plans to eliminate Sudhakar and took up the task of murdering Sudhakar himself before Asif could pull the trigger. Mallesh Anna had repaid his kindness and affection by killing Sudhakar and sacrificed his own life by extracting revenge and saved Asif from committing a crime and murder.

Police and the Turf club security arrived at the scene in minutes. Mallesh Anna was carried to the hospital but he died on the way due to gunshot wounds. Sudhakar Shetty had died a horrible and painful death. Bhaskar survived the attack to live but lost one eye and his face partially scarred.

After the incident Asif left his scooter at the parking lot and ran towards the Haines road cemetery. It was several kilometers but he ran with all his strength towards Jenny's grave and sat stolidly besides her grave. The red wild flower that he had laid on the grave in the morning was still fresh. He closed his eyes, kissed Jenny's grave and suddenly he felt he was breathing much easier. He could feel Jenny's angelic eyes and her heavenly smile as he walked out of the cemetery.

He was now free of revenge but deep down Asif knew he would never be free of Jenny's love.

www.ingramcontent.com/pod-product-compliance
Lightning Source LLC
Chambersburg PA
CBHW030319020726
47493CB00004B/1089